Fitz

A Queer Pride & Prejudice Retelling

Fitz
A Queer Pride & Prejudice Retelling

April Klasen

Independently Published
2024

First Printing: 2024

ISBN 978-0-9944659-8-6

April Klasen
aprilklasenauthor@hotmail.com

Also by April Klasen

Blair: Salem's Daughter
Blair: The Sleeping Daughter
Blair: The Same Daughter
The Annual
Beta
Pure PopAsia
I Heart PopAsia
Summertime Madness
Hook-up or Date

Acknowledgements

The biggest thanks have to go to my critique partner, **Rebecca Trowbridge**. Thank you for suffering through this when Fitz was waaaay whinier than he ended up being. And for guiding me to cut a lot of useless "naval gazing." Your name may have been cursed as I watched my word count drop lower and lower, but then it crawled back up with each added and expanded bit of dialogue, so it all worked out. I trust you. I do.

Thanks has to also go to the costume actor of Mr Wickham at the Jane Austen Centre in Bath, for unwittingly inspiring me to write this story. If you hadn't been a fabulous actor, I would never have had the sudden realisation that Wickham was gay and followed that idea with Darcy being his lover and thus making the betrayal with Georgiana that much worse and oh, yeah, Darcy must've been bisexual. Thank you for the performance and the inspiration.

And finally, thank you *Jane Austen* for the characters and world you created in Pride and Prejudice. You have inspired so many with your works and it is a privilege to get to write my own interpretations of Darcy and Wickham and Lizzie. Though you are dead and have been long enough to render the original copyright null and void, I fully acknowledge that Darcy is your creation.

Chapter three is the smut chapter. Please skip over it or skim it, just DON'T TALK TO ME ABOUT IT! Smut is mentioned a bit in other chapters, but it is nothing like the detailed descriptions you do not need to read in chapter three. As Bek said, "I came to this a gay sex virgin and leave a veteran." I think that was over dramatic, but what would I know, I read too much BL as it is. Just don't, Mother. Please, don't. Or do. Just don't tell me. I really don't want to ever know.

1533 – sodomy laws were introduced during the reign of Henry VIII. Punishment was the death penalty.

1811 to 1820 – Regency period (important to note for the context of this story).

1861 – death penalty was revoked and replaced with a minimum of ten years imprisonment.

1967 – partially legalised same-sex acts between men.

2004 – civil partnership act.

2013 – marriage equality for England.

2014 – marriage equality for Scotland.

2020 – marriage equality for Northern Ireland.

I wish I wasn't writing these dates here like this, because this highlights how fucked up our society has been for centuries and how only recently it has started to make real changes.

"This is Mr Wickham; we've just made his acquaintance!"

Which one of the Bennet girls had spoken? Did I care? Ha. Was I going insane? Dying?! Because my heart had suddenly decided to do the smart thing and run. Escape my chest, though undecided about whether it wanted to claw its way out of my throat... or to drop out my arse and roll away instead. It had to get the hell away from this man staring wide-eyed back at me.

Or else.

Wickham schooled his features into an all too familiar smirk. He gave a quick nod. Courteous. Like you would do to an old acquaintance.

Excuse me?! Who do you think you are? The first time we had seen each other in over a year and… God damn it. This is what you do? Damnation! Damn you George Wickham to hell!

And damn me, too.

Because I, Fitzwilliam Darcy, was still in love with you. How stupid could I be?

"You should invite him to your ball, Mr Bingley," a sickly-sweet voice announced. "You should invite all the officers!"

"Lydia!" someone else snapped in reprimand.

Ball.

Bingley.

George.

Oh no. The panic grew. It swelled and filled my body, setting ever nerve ending on edge. Underneath my seat, my horse shifted restlessly in response. That jolting did not break my eyes from Wickham. Or help that need to flee.

I cannot do this again. No. I was only just able to suffer through life without this man by my side.

And if I was going to have to bear witness yet again to the sickening sight of Wickham romancing ladies. Paying attention to one of the Bennet girls… To Miss Elizabeth...

No.

Just no.

My body reacted for me. Turning the horse with an insistent pull on the reigns and giving her a nudge into action from my heel. She, blessedly, hurried us away.

Vaguely, I could hear Bingley give an apology and follow after me.

I was being rude.

Again.

But there was no way I could have spoken. Not with that man there. Not when I wanted to scream at him again. To beg him to come home. To curse him for ruining everything. Hell, with how crazy I was feeling I also wanted to fall into his arms and sob. Pour it all over him until I was completely empty and did not have to feel it anymore.

Or I just wanted to give him a sound thrashing. Bastard. Fool! Ugh!

So, I ran. Like a coward. Fitzwilliam Darcy ran away from George Wickham.

Once I had made it to the edge of the village, I urged the horse into an outright gallop down the road, muck flying in our wake.

"Darcy!" Bingley called out.

This is ridiculous! We were not meant to cross paths here. Sure, we would eventually have to see each other again, just not in any reality I was willing to accept. Not here or so soon after…

Bastard!

My fists tightened on the reigns.

George, you damned bastard!

How dare he show his face after what he had done. How dare he strut into this part of the country and act like he was so unaffected by his own actions.

"Damn it, Darcy!"

I eased up-right from near lying against the neck of my horse. She responded by slowing, heaving gasps of air. Funny, so was I.

"Good heavens, man." The sudden impact of Bingley's hand on my shoulder finally jolted me, bringing me back to this body and to this time. "What was that about?"

I shook my head to clear it. "I… Sorry…"

"Darcy," Bingley squeezed my shoulder. "Breathe." He demonstrated with a deep inhale and then releasing.

Looking at my friend, I followed his lead. Inhale… exhale… inhale… exhale…

I came to realise I was shaking and… what the hell? Was I crying? This was ridiculous! I was Fitzwilliam

Darcy! A gentleman! Not some love sick teen with a broken heart.

How am I not over this?!

"It's fine, Darcy," Bingley drew his horse closer and leant over. Hand shifting from shoulder to back of neck, he pulled me into an awkward half embrace.

And that did it. I collapsed into him and sobbed.

Anyone else and I would have rather died. But I had been that shoulder. That ear to listen to his sobbed words of grief and fear of having to step up and fill his father's shoes. Bingley was never going to judge me for this.

I pulled back, wiped a kerchief over my face; we were too near Netherfield for this outburst. What would the neighbours say?

"Sorry."

"Do not be. But, why?" Bingley asked.

I could not meet his eyes at all. "I didn't think I'd ever see him again."

"Who? That Wickham chap? He did look rather familiar. Who is he?"

Who is Wickham?

Who is George?

Well, that was easy. George had been… everything. Lord, can I be that pathetic?

*

It had always been Fitz and George. Thicker than thieves. As boys, we would spend almost every waking hour together playing, hunting, and trailing our tutor around. I loved George as a brother.

I wanted nothing more than for us to always be together and share everything. And I believed that was how it would always be. We would grow up and I would become the next master of Pemberley and George would be there beside me. Always.

Always side by side.

But love changes.

And from best friends, we shifted towards something more when we were just twelve.

"Fitz!" George hollered.

That was the only warning I received. I was tackled to the ground, landing with a thump, air forced from my lungs as the full weight of George landed on top. "Ugh," I groaned.

Grinning George sat up on my stomach. "Gotcha!"

"Get off of me!" I tried to roll him off, but could not move at all with him sitting there. So, I reached up to fight. Our hands grappled, slapped, poked, pinched, and then finally, tickled.

George rolled to the side and tried his best to defend against my fingers.

I showed no mercy. I clamoured on top of the other boy and dug my wiggling fingers into the most vulnerable parts; neck, arm pits, belly.

George howled. "Noooooo! Ahhhhh! Stop. Fitz!" His feet kicked the ground.

"Do you surrender?!" I giggled my demand.

"Never!"

And so I went back in and attacked harder.

No one tried to stop this. For one, it was normal for the residents of Pemberly to witness our roughhousing. And… right in this moment… we were alone in the far reaches of the garden. Shrubbery blocking us from view from the house.

I started to realise how close we were. And I liked it.

I liked George.

It had started to grow slowly, in a way I never even noticed that I went from wanting to play with my best friend to… well.

I wanted to touch him, like hold his hand, hug him, and to…

While he was still laughing and crying, I leant forward and brushed my closed lips over George's fat rosy cheek.

Silence.

I pulled back to look at George's reaction.

We stared at each other. I waited to see what would happen. Would he push me off and tell me he hated me?

"Why'd you do that?" He asked instead.

"Dunno. Wanted to," I shrank back, shoulders hunching. The way I tended to always do whenever there were new people around. Trying to be the smallest there so I would be over looked and not asked questions.

But George knew what I was doing. He reached up and grabbed onto the collar of my shirt and yanked me back down. Our closed lips smashed together.

Oh.

OH!

This time when I withdrew, George releasing me, I collapsed to the side. I rolled so I was laying on my back on the grass beside George.

Heart pounding.

Face starting to burn.

And a grin.

An uncontrollable grin pulling at my lips.

Lips that had kissed George.

"You sap," George pinched my cheek. "You really do love me."

Love?

Maybe that was what this was. More than like. This was way more than liking him.

I grinned harder.

George shuffled closer so our shoulders were touching.

And, without hesitating, I grabbed his hand and held it.

"Fitz is in love," he sang. Over and over. Even when I rolled back to face him and we scrapped for a while.

But I could not deny the tease. So, to get George to stop, I kissed him again. And again. And again. Soon, George was kissing me back. These cute little pecks on our lips. Until we had dissolved into fits of giggling.

"And?" I questioned.

"And what?"

"Do you love me?" I asked uncertainly.

I watched as bright red stained George's baby fat cheeks and he mumbled in response. "'course I do, Fitz. Idiot."

I buried my face into George's neck, following as he squirmed and yelled about my nose tickling him. But I wanted to do this. To cuddle and touch. It felt good.

In the end, we got up, bumping shoulders with each step, and started to walk back to the grand house.

Our clothes were a mess, grass looked to be staining our breeches. "Oh! You two will be the death of me!" the old house keeper scolded as she looked over our appearance. "Go on! Up to your rooms and get cleaned up. You better be presentable for dinner time with the master and mistress this evening!"

I loved the gentle hand that brushed through my wild dark curls as she ordered us around. "Yes, ma'am." I leant into the touch for a moment.

"Go on!" she ordered with a smile.

George raced me up the stairs and down the halls to the nursery. We barrelled in, squeezing through the doorway pressed against each other.

"Shhh," the nurse maid hissed from her post in the rocking chair, her finger pressed against her pursed lips.

Both of us froze and glanced at the bassinet beside her.

Georgiana. So tiny. But so so loud when she was unhappy. Little princess. Too many times she had screamed and told the whole household that we were doing something we should not have been doing. A tattletale, even as a babe. Luckily, she slept on still.

More conscious of our sounds, we went to the room we shared. It had made sense to the adults to place us into the nursery together. Especially since George's mother had died.

It so happened that we were very happy to be joined at the hip all of our childhood.

And it seemed as if we would be the only ones to ever use the nursery. No siblings. That was until Georgiana had been born.

Then, it felt odd for us boys to be sharing with a new born. We were twelve, growing fast. Already, shirts and waistcoats had gotten tighter. Hems of our breachers were crawling up our legs and exposing more of our stockings. We were almost teenagers.

But our sleeping arrangements would not change yet. Packed and sitting at the foot of our beds sat two travel trunks. Boarding school.

We stripped off our soiled clothes and splashed each other with water from the hip basin in the corner of the room. Drying off we fussed over who got to wear what.

"No, I want to wear the blue."

"You wore it yesterday."

"It suits me better."

"But it's my favourite colour."

"That's a lie, you like green better."

Which meant we decided with a game of rock, paper, scissors. Though George won, he decided to wear the green.

When called for dinner, we came down quietly, greeted Father as he came in, and moved to stand behind our seats and wait.

Mother glided into the room and smiled at us. "Good evening, boys."

"Good evening, ma'am."

"Good evening, Mother."

She took her seat at one end of the table and the men of the room took theirs. Father sitting at the opposite end and us boys side by side in the middle.

I tried to shrink in my seat, especially when Mother asked questions about our day. "What did you two do today?"

Umm…

George answered for me. He entertained her with a wild tale of our adventures in the garden. Appeased Father that we had practiced our Latin a little even though we had no tutor anymore.

I ate in silence and watched George. I liked doing that. George told amazing stories. He had even put on voices and acted out parts.

"Anything to add, Fitzwilliam?" my father asked.

No. "Pardon, sir?" I turned around and tried not to gape at my father.

Mr Darcy gave a warm smile. "I asked if there was anything you wanted to add to this exciting tale."

Oh, please do not everyone look at me and wait for something interesting to come out of my mouth. I panicked. "I wrote a letter to cousin," I said.

I was not going to tell my parents about kissing George. That was something precious for me to cherish and… I did not want to share it. I wanted hoard it. Keep it to myself.

And I noticed George had left that part out of his story

We ate. My parents spoke. My mother told us about a letter she had received from Lady Catherine de Bourgh. "She was disappointed that we did not go to summer with her at Rosings this year."

Father chuckled into his claret.

"Of course, she has demanded we promise to come for winter," Mother said.

"Have you written her back yet, my dear?"

Mother smirked as she popped a fresh berry into her mouth.

As if he already knew, Father laughed.

I watched this exchange in fascination. This. This was how husband and wife were to act. This was love.

"I'm so happy you boys are going to school together," Mother said.

George had gotten bored and slipped off his shoe. Stockinged foot snaked over and poked at my calf.

Trying my best not to attract attention, I slipped my hands from the table and reached over to pinch George's thigh.

He kicked me back and wriggled his toes over my ankle.

Father laughed. "Ah yes. I see what you mean, my dear."

I did not see it. So, I frowned at my elders. What did they see? Had they been able to tell that I loved him as more than my friend? I was not ready for them to know that, yet!

Mother took pity and smiled indulgently. "You are such good friends, more like brothers. It will be good for you both to depend upon each other when you are so far away from home."

Like brothers?

Under the table, George hooked his foot over my ankle as if he was holding my hand.

"Don't worry boys," Father reassured. "Boarding school is a rite of passage for all gentlemen. We've all gone through it."

Right. Living and studying with a large group of strangers was a trial and tribulation we had to pass before becoming adults.

I shifted in my seat uncomfortably.

Father had said something like that all year round. Our tutor had given us his horror stories. Upperclassmen being tyrants, having to share beds in the dorms, food being inedible…

"And," Father continued. "When you have someone with you, it cements your bond for life."

"I promise, Mr Darcy," George finally spoke. "I'll look after Fitzwilliam."

I did not like how that sounded. "I'll look after you too," I blurted out in irritation.

"Of course, you will," George snapped back. "What the hell?"

"George," Father warned.

He cringed. "My apologies," he nodded to both of my parents for the slip up. Under the table, he kicked me once more.

I kicked back.

Soon, it was very obvious that we were not sitting still, each hit jolting us to sit upright and glare at each other.

A long-suffering sigh and my father excused us from the table.

I stood quickly. George took a little longer, slipping his shoe back on before he too stood. We bowed. And then we fled. Pushing and shoving as we hurried out.

Later, when we dressed for bed, my parents came to the nursery to bid us goodnight. Mother kissed us both on the forehead. Father waited for her to leave and go to Georgiana before sitting on the end of my bed and looking very serious.

George shared an apprehensive look with me.

"I don't want to alarm you," Father said. "But you need to prepare for this. School isn't going to be a pleasant place. But it is a necessary experience." He focussed on me in particular. "It's going to push you out of your comfort zone and force you to become a man."

I tried my best not to look down. Please, Father, do not be disappointed in me. I want to make you proud. I want to be a man like you.

He looked to George. "I wished I had had a friend going in with me for the first time. You are going to be all each other has initially." He smiled, as if he was remembering things. "But then you are going to make so many friends. And the friends you make now, will follow you into the rest of your lives, boys. Make sure you choose well with whom you align with. Being friends with those with 'power' in school does not mean they will have power outside. In fact, most of those end up alienating many because they abuse that power."

The silence that followed, did not need to be filled with anything else. I sat and thought about what we had been told.

My father stood. Ruffled my hair and George's before leaving, taking the candle with him and closing the door over.

"Are you scared?" George asked in the darkness.

"Not sure," I answered honestly. "I do not want to do anything wrong and disappoint my father. What if…" my words fell off.

A shuffling filled the night and then my bed dipped.

George wiggled under the covers with me, our toes and knees bumped. I reached up and mapped out the shapes of his face, squeezing his nose and laughing when he smacked my hand away. He bumped his forehead to mine. Hot breath blew over my face.

"We'll look out for each other."

"Promise?"

"Of course!"

We hooked our pinkie fingers.

"It's going to fine, Fitz," he nuzzled his nose against mine.

Impulsively, I pushed further and kissed him.

As long as he was by my side, I would not worry. Everything would be fine. And we would be happy.

That is it. I, Fitzwilliam Darcy, hated George Wickham. He could disappear for all I cared. Along with the rest of the idiots at school.

School was hell. Too many boys squeezed in together. Meals in the mess hall around the long tables saw elbows in faces and arguments over food stealing. We were at each other's throats over the smallest things.

Then there were the upper-class men, enjoying the torment they forced upon us. The blatant harassment. Giving pointless orders we were not allowed to refuse only to waste our time and make us late to our lessons. Name calling and teasing of anything from stammered speech to unconventional noses.

They enjoyed targeting my quietness. Sniffed it out immediately. Shrinking and hiding was impossible.

And George, at first, tried to protect me.

At first.

Then George pulled back. He no longer sat beside me, pressed in so close we were thigh to thigh and shoulder to shoulder. He no longer leant in close and smiled.

He no longer called me Fitz.

George made new friends.

I was alone.

Every so often, I would hear snickers. Looking over, I would find George and his cronies, and they would try to stifle it. But I knew it had been at my expense.

My stomach would churn. And I would turn away and ignore them.

A lot of my time was spent hiding. When you are quiet, it is easy to slip away. I found a lot of places disused or out of the way. One such place, was a storage room in a tower. Obviously, it was in a restricted area. But I went anyway. Explored the sheet covered furniture. Sat and read.

It hurt.

I hated being there.

And… I hated what I was seeing myself become.

My father had told me this place would help make me into a man. Yet, I ran away and hid and tried to be as small as possible.

Was this the kind of man I would always be?

"Poor little Darcy," George mocked as I entered the dorm room in the middle of the day. I needed a text book. But what he was doing there… He laid sprawled over my little cot bed and in his hands…

"Put that down!" I demanded.

He smirked as he sat upright and waved the letter around. "Dear Father, I am sorry to disappoint you," he started to read aloud.

I launched at him, tackling him so hard, we tumbled over the other side of the bed and onto the floor with a thump. We wrestled, and then dissolved into childish scraps. Pulling hair, slaps, and yanking clothes. In our struggle, my letter home tore.

Good.

Let it be destroyed.

I would never write like that again.

Never show how weak I was on record.

I let out a guttural yell before shoving George back and standing up right. Taking the pieces of the letter, I shoved it deep into my pockets. I would find a fire to completely destroy it all, later.

George laughed.

I looked down at him on the floor. Hair and clothes a mess. Some scratches to his face.

"Why?!" Burst out before I could think.

He sat up, rested his arm on one bent knee. "Why what, Darcy?"

"Why did you change to be this?" I snarled back.

He shrugged. "Better than being like you."

It stabbed. "Do you think I enjoy being this..." my voice broke. A sharp squeak. Damn it.

He laughed at that.

I kicked him and started to storm off.

Behind me, I heard scuffling and then George's hand was heavy on my shoulder. "Darcy."

"Stop it!" I snapped. "Wickham," came as an afterthought.

He broke into a laugh. A real one. Watching his face crumple from that awful smirk and back into something real. George-like. I smiled soft.

"Look, I'm-" he broke off.

"All boys!" an upper-class man's voice echoed. "Come to the great hall! Now!"

Oh no. Those words sounded like they were getting closer. Along with the click of heels on the floorboards. Shit!

"Shit. We have to hide." George shoved at my back, trying to hurry me out of the hall without being seen by our sadistic upper-class men.

I, not thinking, grabbed George's hand and led the way. "I know a spot," was all I said.

George followed. He did not take his hand back and I did not release it.

We made our way into the restricted area, which was empty at that time of the day. Down and around, through an old door and up the winding stone spiral staircase. Our hurried steps echoed.

Part way up, I pushed open a door and pulled George inside.

But I kept moving us on.

"Why not here?" George whispered, looking around in confusion.

I tugged on his hand. "I know a better spot." And it was better than this empty space. On the other side was another door and in there, disused furniture sat under dust cloths. In fact, there was a very lumpy lounge that was more comfortable than sitting on the floor.

I pushed open the door…

And froze.

Two boys sat on the lounge, kissing each other on the lips.

Smith and Johnson. Upper-class men in their final years. They were cradling each other's face gently. Eyes closed, and head tilted so they slotted together perfectly. Lost in each other.

I stared in horror… and fascination. We were not the only ones.

Crash!

I jumped and turned to see the avalanche of junk George had spilled. George cringed. "Sorry," he whispered.

Looking back over, Smith and Johnson had leapt apart and stared at us, the intruders. Smith rose to his feet. "I should take you both outside for a sound thrashing!" He growled.

Without a word or anything I yanked George back through the door.

The upper-class men both yelled at us to wait.

But I hurried, started to run as we made it to the stairs.

"Darcy!" George yanked on my hand, forcing me to stop on the step below to look up at him.

God he was beautiful and…

No thought, I leant up, rising to my toes. Eyes focused on his lips. Mine parting. Oh God. An inch away, George reacted.

"What are you doing?!" he stumbled back. "Are you… are you trying to kiss me?!"

I rocked back, heels hitting the stone step. Oh shit. Oh no. No no no… I released his hand fast and did the only thing I could think of. I ran.

Like a coward.

"Fitz!"

Bloody Hell!

"Fitzwilliam!"

I slowed at the bottom step and waited, head hanging. I am such a damn idiot!

Here it comes. I listened to the rushed *tap tap tap* of his shoes before he was on the step above. "What…"

The door to the stairs in front of us opened and a teacher narrowed his eyes. "Mr Darcy and Mr Wickham. My office. Now!"

Ashamed of being caught, we followed with our faces downcast. After the lecture about being in restricted areas, we slunk out of the office. Stinging skin from our punishments.

George jerked his head up, and strode away, confident. He left me behind.

And my heart broke. A real physical ache radiated in my chest and I lifted my hand to press against it. As if I was staunching the blood of a wound. As if I would mend it and be back to normal.

What had I done?

*

The next day, I sat in the library with my Latin studies before me.

George sat at a table of boys all talking in whispers and snorting laughs.

Neither of us had spoken to each other since the incident. I was accepting this as our new normal. If George wanted nothing to do with me because I had tried to do something unacceptable… then I would honour that. I would respect George and stay away.

"Wickham!"

I startled, eyes bugging out, shoulders hitting my ears. Twisting to see the upper-class man poking his head in through the library door. Beckoning George over with a wave. There were a series of shushes that followed. The upper-class man ignored them; did not yell again.

George stood up from the table of boys and strode over. Confidence clear in his straight back, chin held high, and cheeky smirk.

He did not look my way as he passed by.

Ignored.

Great. I slumped in my chair and picked up my book once more. It is not like we had never fought before… but that was easier to bear with than this. Fighting over broken toys and mean words were simple. Normal.

Why did I try to kiss George?! What made me think that my affection would have been accepted? That George would have returned it after so long without? Would have kissed me back and we could have lived happily ever after?

God, I was a fool! An utter fool!

There was something wrong with me. I turned the page in the book, not reading a single word. Trapped with my thoughts and no way to escape them, so I made sure no one else knew. Acted like I was being normal. Not that anyone paid me attention.

A normal day in hell.

*

Time passed. I learned to utilise my silence. It became my armour. I did not have to let anyone in and talk to them. I could stare at them until they became uncomfortable and left, I could ignore. Rise above. When you do not talk with others easily, silence is seen as snobbery and they avoid you. And honestly, I actually preferred the solitude to the inane natter. The gossiping. The insults.

Well, that was not the absolute truth.

I missed George.

Missed his easy banter and little teases. And missed having him to buffer. I could always suffer through conversations when George would do the talking for us both. Watching him and listening. He was great at telling stories.

Now, that would never happen again.

After all, why would he want me around when his new friends were better company. They could talk normally. Could have a proper laugh. Did not make things awkward and try to kiss George… or perhaps they did and he was more receptive to them. Damn it. I do not know.

It is better this way.

Better if I…

I am a gentleman. I… had to act like a gentleman.

*

New boys arrived with the start of a new school year.

In the batch of fresh meat was Charles Bingley. Gangly youth, way too eager to please others, stumbled over his tongue as much as he did his feet.

"Um… hello?" Bingley's voice squeaked.

I looked up from my bowl of bland porridge. "Hello?"

"Is it okay if I sit here?"

Hardly any space on the edge of the bench beside me. I frowned and looked down the rest of the table. There were plenty of bigger spaces.

I scooted over to give more room and nodded.

He sighed in relief and plopped down, bowl and spoon clattering on the scarred table top. "Thanks. No one else was letting me sit."

"Don't ask for permission," I told him.

"Huh?"

I went back to my food. "Do not ask for permission to sit. Sit wherever you want and force them to accept you there."

"But," he wiped the back of his hand over his mouth. "That's not how you make friends."

I shrugged. "I do not have any friends. But if you want to survive here, you need to stop being so polite."

"Oh."

Ugh. That hurt. The same way you hear the whine of a dog that was being kicked and you had to do something and stop it.

Bingley hunched over and poked at his porridge with his spoon. A little suspicious of it.

"Do you… read?" What kind of question was that? I was an idiot. A complete simpleton! Read? Was that how one started conversation with strangers now?

"Huh?" his eyes came up to mine. "Like novels?"

I nodded, not willing to trust my mouth again.

He shook his head. "Father says novels are all filth. He will not allow my sisters to read any, either."

"He isn't wrong," I said, as if I had read more than a handful of novels. "How many sisters do you have?"

Bingley tipped his head to the side. "Are you trying to be my friend?"

"Yes." I forced out the word. Not knowing why I would try and befriend this boy. If I actually wanted to be friends with him or if I wanted to make this one interaction not so terrible.

He brightened. Sat up straight and smiled at me and started to babble away. He asked me questions and actually listened to my responses.

He was… interesting.

I did not show him hiding spots, that felt a little too personal to be sharing with someone I just met. But I did make sure he did not get lost. And made sure the upper-class men did not give him useless orders.

Bingley made other friends.

I prepared for the inevitable. He too would leave me behind and I would be alone, again. But that did not happen. He balanced everything perfectly. His new friends and me. On occasion, he would see me and would accept a nod as his only acknowledgement.

"Why do you talk to Darcy?" someone asked Bingley. "He's such a bore."

I waited, hidden from their sight, because I too wanted to know.

"Because he is my friend." Simple. Innocent. It amazed me.

And it made what happened with George hurt even more. Or maybe I needed to not try and kiss anymore of my friends.

Not that I wanted to.

George was the only one I wanted to do that with.

*

Home for the holidays was… uneasy. The first time we went home, George acted the same with my parents. He told them tales about school.

Father looked over to me when he realised, none of these stories included me.

The second time home, my cousin was visiting so I followed him around the grounds and into town when he went. He returned to university and I went back to boarding school.

This time home, I did not see George except for meals. I spent time in my new room where I had complete privacy, roaming the grounds, or in the nursery with Georgiana. She had grown so fast and was babbling in broken English about anything and everything.

Father pulled me aside one morning after breakfast. I followed him to his office. "Yes, sir?"

"Is everything alright?" he waved me to sit on the lounge as he went to the side board and poured two glasses of liquor.

I frowned as he offered one to me. As he continued to hold it out, I took it into my hands, hesitantly.

He sat on the edge of his desk and waited for my response.

I tried to sip the amber liquor, coughed and spluttered as I tasted it. Yuck! Awful! Why did anyone drink this? Why did my father keep it in his study?

He chuckled into his glass.

"I made a friend," I said.

"Bingley?" he asked.

I nodded.

"You mentioned him in your letters. Is there anything else?"

I shrugged. "It is not a nice place. But I am surviving," I assured him.

Mr Darcy watched me.

I stared back, the same way I did to people at school. Blank. Unconcerned.

"I know you're not very good at talking with people you do not know," he admitted. "And school has shown you how not to treat others."

I snorted.

He smiled. "But you're growing up fine, Fitzwilliam."

"I don't think so," I mumbled and tried to cover it by drinking more of the awful stuff. Maybe he had given it to me to loosen my tongue or because it gave me something to hold and use as a cover.

"Why do you say that?"

I hung my head. I did not want to disappoint him. "I feel like I'm a coward and..." the words froze in my mouth.

"Does this have to do with George not being your friend anymore?"

My head snapped up and I gaped at my father.

He sipped his drink and again waited for me.

"A little," I admitted. A lot, was what I should have said.

Silence.

Then, Father rose up and took my glass from my hands. He threw it back. "Well, you need to be a man in this situation and face George. Go and talk to him."

Sorry, Father, but I cannot do that. George hates me. He is not my friend anymore because he knows I love him and even though he was receptive to my affections before, he is not anymore. I am respecting that decision by not going anywhere near him. So, no. No can do.

I was thankful that twelve-year-old me had hoarded my feelings. The very thought of admitting them to my father left me wondering how he would react. If he would look at me different… send George away? Send me away?

"Fitzwilliam," he used his stern tone. The one that said there was no room for argument.

I sighed and rose to my feet. A quick bow and I went off to do my father's bidding.

I did not know what I was going to say to George or if he was going to want to talk to me. Maybe I could convince him to be civil with me in front of my family, so they would not ask questions again. Or he would laugh at me for following orders.

I found George in the garden with Georgiana and the nursemaid. He had her on his back and was 'galloping' around for her. She shrieked with laughter and clung to his neck.

"Master Fitzwilliam," the nursemaid announced me. "Have you come to play, also?"

Georgiana's head swung round to find me. A fist full of George's hair and she tugged him to turn. "Fitz! Fitz! Fitz!" she screamed, little legs kicking.

"Ouch!" George hurried over to me, to offer her up.

I took her into my arms.

She sat upright and started to babble away. Words here and there I could understand. George. Horsey. Yay!

I smiled at her and nodded for her to continue.

Soon, she was wiggling and the nursemaid came and took her. "Aye, it's time to go inside," she bobbed a curtsey and left.

I turned to George. "Um…" I cleared my throat. "I actually came to speak to you."

He raised a brow.

"In private," I added. No point in having servants over hear something that might slip out in the heat of the moment. I knew we were not going to be able to have a calm and rational discussion. After all, this was us.

George nodded his head at a path leading towards the far reaches of the gardens.

He started to walk and I followed.

Come on, Fitzwilliam, think! Think of a way to explain it without making this worse.

Once we had reached the furthest point of the garden and were unseen by the house, George turned on me. Chin lifted and smirk in place. "What do you want, Darcy?"

I gritted my teeth.

"Well?" he pushed.

"I…"

"Come on, out with it!"

"Stop that."

"Stop what?"

"Stop pushing me!" I snapped back.

He rolled his eyes. "Get over it."

I stepped forward, my chest puffed out.

He mimicked me.

We snarled at each other. Horrible words. Then all a sudden, I shoved him back. He threw a punch. And we scuffled until I was able to knock him to the ground and scream at him. "I GET IT! I FUCKING GET IT, GEORGE! YOU HATE ME! I'M DISGUSTING!"

He sat up in the dirt and gaped, a black eye blooming. "Fitz."

"BUT…" I gasped for air. "All I ever wanted was to love you," I finished.

And there it was.

The words I knew I did not want to admit again to him. It would have been less humiliating and exposing to admit that my father sent me to talk to him. Damn it!

Then I was on my arse. George yanked my ankle and sent me sprawling to the ground. I did not give him any opportunity to gain the upper hand. Always moving, always snarling and fighting back. Too many fights in school had me well practiced.

Finally, George gripped my face hard, fingers digging into my cheeks as he yanked me around and held me in place.

Then he kissed me.

Hard and messy.

An angry kiss.

Pulling back, he breathed heavy into my open mouth. "I love you, Fitz! Christ!" Shoving, he released me and flopped onto his back.

I stared at him in utter shock.

We were both gasping for air.

"What the devil?!" I demanded.

George grunted.

"You… then… why? Why have you been treating me like you hated me?"

He laughed meanly.

I kicked at his thigh in retaliation.

He sat up and threw dirt at me. "Fool. It was easier than letting you get us caught!"

"What?"

"Ugh," he rolled his eyes. "If we acted like normal someone would have found out and then we would have been in trouble. Get it?!"

I did. But it did not mean that what he had done had not hurt. "So, you thought to make this decision without telling me?! Being one of the main reasons why I have felt like shit for years?!"

George stared at me.

I leant my arms onto my propped-up knees. "Father sent me to talk to you because he noticed we weren't friends anymore."

George finally looked away.

"We can't keep doing this," I told him.

"It was working," he snapped back.

"And then what? We go our separate ways when we get to university and never speak again?"

"Maybe," he admitted.

"That's horseshit!"

"And how did you want it to go? We act all lovey dovey and then are caught and have to flee the country? There is no place for what we are, Fitz! Or it could be worse, we could end up swinging from the gallows. You forget that this is not two kids kissing and knowing no better. We are almost adults."

"Who would have to know?!"

"What?"

"Who would have to know?" I repeated. "We are childhood friends, that is going to of course make us closer than most. My father has all but adopted you into the family. No-one can question that we are connected and important to each other."

He stared at me like I was crazy.

"What we do behind closed doors isn't anyone's business." I swallowed. "I want to try, George. I want to try and have a little bit of happiness in my life."

"And if we're caught?"

I shook my head. "I won't let us be."

"You think that people will accept that we are 'really good friends' as a reason?"

"Childhood friends. Like brothers," I corrected. "And yes. They will not know."

I waited for him.

"Or," I offered him the other option, his option. "We go back to not talking and let everyone think we hate each other and…" I die on the inside again. "Your choice."

"Why is it my choice?" he snapped back.

"Because I already have chosen. I want to love you."

As if I was twisting his arm and forcing him into it, he groaned and collapsed back. "Fine."

"Really?" I asked, hopeful.

"Yes. We cannot always keep this up anyway. Everyone here acts all confused because we are not talking like we use to."

"We can be civil when we are at Pemberly. If that is how you want to do it." I offered.

"Nah," he rolled over and propped his head on his hand and stared at me. "I've missed you, Fitz."

I kissed him, exactly how I had been dying to do so for a long time. And he kissed me back.

Our shared room had a lock. Once we were inside and there was no possible reason for anyone else to come or for us to leave, I locked the door. The click sound sent anticipation flying up my spine.

"Hmm," George smirked from the other side of the room. "Calling it an early night, Fitz?"

"It has been a long day," I played along. "We should be getting to bed." Walking towards him, I started to loosen my cravat and pull it free from my neck.

"Oh yes," his body moulded into mine as we pressed together. "To bed immediately." He wrapped his arms around my neck and kissed me hard.

My hands trailed all over his body. Gripping his waist and yanking his shirt. Skimming his stomach as I unbuttoned his breeches. I scraped my nails up and down his thighs to feel him shudder.

"Uh, Fitz," his breathy sigh fed into the burning desire to be on him.

We had convinced everyone we were just childhood friends. Every casual arm over the shoulder, cheeky grin shot across the room. Spending almost every waking moment together was always seen as innocent. When it meant so much more to us. It was a promise of love and affection and… more. Just more to come.

So far, we had kissed and fumbled and brought a quick release of pleasure to each other. Always hidden. Always vigilant. Always a little less than what we needed.

Now, we were at university and sharing a room together. Alone.

And there was nothing going to stop us from experiencing what we had been dying to do.

Giggling into each other's mouths, we stripped to be completely naked. Skin on skin. My lips followed my hands. Dropped kisses reverently onto George's shoulders, his sternum, his ribs… lower still.

George plunged his fingers into my hair and pulled me back to his mouth.

"Bed," George pleaded.

We landed and rolled, wrestled to be the one on top. Each movement rubbed us together and elicited moans.

Finally, George settled above me. I planted my left foot on the bed beside his hip and urged mine up. He bared down onto me. We found a rhythm. A rise and fall.

His hands gripped the sheets by my head.

I reached down and took his and mine into my fists and rubbed them together. Stroking up and down, against each other, bringing on shudders and gasps of names.

"Fitz," George groaned and pushed down harder into me. Grinding.

"George!" I gasped.

Even with this privacy, we knew we had to be as silent as possible. Neighbouring rooms could hear. It would take little effort to figure out why we were repeating each other's names like frantic prayers.

Silent love making.

That was our curse.

George dipped his head and pressed his lips to my throat.

Silent was going to be impossible.

I bit my lip hard to stop it, but deep in my throat I groaned, the wet kisses against soft skin sent me spiralling.

He whispered. "Fuuuuuck Fitz. Fuck. I love you. Love you. Fitz."

My legs wrapped around his waist and drew him in even tighter. My hands were too much of an obstacle in the tight space between. They came up and instead landed on his back, scratching and stroking.

We rubbed together in a frenzy. But it was not quite enough. "Hand. Fitz," he begged.

I slipped it back between.

He moved to be on his forearms and give more room.

Focussing on the heads, my fingers skimmed over the slits and gripped on each downward pull of hips.

There.

There!

In the hot channel of my palm, my release shot up and over my chest.

In a state of bliss, I loosened my grip on myself and tightened my hand for George to hurry and find his end there. He tucked his chin and moaned, hips stuttering, and made a mess on top of mine.

Then collapsed.

"Ugh," I grunted at the impact.

Our hearts raced, beating so hard that we felt them as we were chest to chest. His laboured breath hit my neck. And it was sticky between us.

"Love you, George," I whispered.

This was heaven.

*

Did we attend lectures and study in the library? I think so. Did I retain any information? Clearly not. The only things I knew, cared to learn about, never happened in a classroom.

Once that door closed and that lock clicked, we were on each other. We gave into every impulse. I learned everything about his body. Where to bite to have him shiver, where to suck to leave love marks so he knew who loved him, how he tasted, heavy on my tongue.

We did everything.

All those tid bits of information we had heard, every last 'did you know' we tested out.

Nothing was off limits. Because we knew no better. We had nothing to compare this to. It was us feeding into the crazy need to get as close to each other as we could.

One day, George came home with a bottle of oil.

"Planning on cooking?" I asked.

He locked the door. "Strip," he ordered.

I raised a brow. And then frowned. "Where are you going to use that?"

"Strip and I'll show you."

Naked, because from that impish look on his face, I trusted that this was going to feel amazing, I laid on my stomach.

He ran his fingers up and down my spine, dropped kisses to muscles there that took his fancy. Then started to massage the cheeks of my arse.

"I don't see where the oil comes in," I murmured.

He gave my arse a slap. It stung. But also felt… pleasurable. I moaned. A quick surprised moan.

George froze. "You liked that?"

"Shut up," my face burned. I buried it into the pillow I was gripping.

Testing, as if this was an experiment, he slapped again. The crack of skin on skin rang out… along with my echoed groan. It made me throb and ache.

Why was this so hot?

George chuckled. "You are full of surprises, Fitz."

"Fuck you," I snapped.

"Maybe later."

I perked up at that. We had yet to do anything penetrative. Of course, we had heard of how two men could. That was always thrown around in sneers, as insults. I had listened, careful and always thinking, how? Churning the idea over and over. How did that fit in there? Why? Would it be pleasurable? Or was it such a shameful thing? Would I be… dirtied, because of it? Not that I could ask for details, for advice.

All I could do was collect the information and share it with George's pieces he had gathered. But we had yet to test it out.

Then, George spread my cheeks and drizzled the oil.

I jolted.

"Don't move," he insisted.

"And how am I meant to do that?!" I was completely focused on the single digit now rubbing and circling. Moving closer and closer, now over the tight furl of muscles.

Halting, George waited.

I held my breath.

He waited more.

The oil slipped and coated my bullocks. I squirmed.

"Do you want to stop?" he asked quietly.

I gritted my teeth. "No. I want you, George."

"Are you sure?"

"Damn it," I snapped, about ready to turn around and yell at him to shove his whole hand in already.

And he moved. One finger pushed past the tight rim and… oh… that was not… I shifted.

"Talk to me, Fitz."

"It's…" I struggled to find the words and not lose the mood. "It is a finger in my arse, George. Nothing special."

"Oh," he sounded disappointed. "Do you want to stop and go back to normal?"

I shrugged.

When he introduced a second finger… it made me squirm and wonder why anyone would want to do this. It burned and ached. Hissing, I looked over my shoulder to him. "Are you doing this right?"

George frowned at himself; eyes fixated on where he was penetrating me. "If you're not enjoying it, I guess not."

"Want to keep trying and see if it improves?" I suggested.

George chewed on his bottom lip. "What do you want?"

"You," I said without hesitation.

He grinned and leaned in. Close. Biting my shoulder, kissing my neck, sucking hard and leaving hickeys. It felt good. So good. I groaned and ground my hips into the bed for the friction.

While he was teasing me with his mouth, his fingers moved, they scissored and stretched and opened me up.

"Better?" he murmured against my neck.

"Somewhat," I was not sure if what we were leading to was going to work. If it was going to feel good at all.

Careful, he pulled out his fingers and the sudden emptiness left me… "George," I whined.

"What is it?"

"I don't know, put something back in."

He chuckled at that. "Give me a second." Stripped and climbing onto the bed, he positioned himself. His cock bumped into the meat of my buttocks.

Oh.

"Are you still sure of this?" his hand rested on my lower back, hot and sticky.

"Yes," I swallowed as his head nestled between my cheeks and started to push.

It hurt.

He was bigger than two fingers.

Much bigger than that.

I gritted my teeth and buried my head into the pillow to muffle any strange sounds I was making. His hands rubbed my back and thighs, soothing, in big strokes.

Then he choked out. "Fuuuuuuuck… Fitz… Hmmm."

Oh.

It hurt for me. But felt good for him. I could endure it if he was getting pleasure from it.

"You're so tight," he muttered.

Slow, he sank in. And then, he bottomed out. His thighs rested against the back of mine.

He paused to let me adjust.

Slipping his hips back, he withdrew, slipped forward, and pushed back inside.

"Huh," a shiver flew up my spine. That had been… pleasurable. Somewhat.

"Talk… to me… Fitz," a broken demand.

"I do not know. It feels awkward and like I am too full but when you moved it felt good," I babbled.

That encouraged him and he moved again. Soft little rocks. Gentle.

It still burned. But there was something about it… something. Oh, dear god, hmm…

George dropped his chest to my back and laid fully on top. That! "Oh, yes," I groaned. His weight bearing down and the gentle thrusts. My brain was overwhelmed by sensations.

He kissed and chewed on my neck.

"Can you get up on your knees?" he asked.

Knees? What were those again?

He sat back. It terrified me that he was going to pull out completely. I pushed back onto him and got my knees up under me partly. His impatient hands moved me the rest of the way. My head stayed down, biting into the pillow.

And that is when we found it. The angle he was working, even with his gentle rocking, went deeper. Stroked something inside. Something I never knew existed.

"Hey, are alright?" he slowed. Soothing hands returned to my sides.

"Keep doing it," I demanded. How dare he halt?!

More direct hits on this sweet spot and the pleasure that came over me rolled and crashed and ugh, fuck… fuck!

George quickened his thrusts. Short and sharp. Slapping skin on skin filled our room.

God, I did not care if anyone heard us now.

My cock ached.

"Fitz… hmmm. Mine. My love, my love, my love," he chanted. Reaching around, he took me in hand and stroked in time with his thrusts.

That finished me and I screamed into the pillow.

George moaned. "Shit, you're getting tighter on me, Fitz." Then quick to follow me into bliss.

*

The words of my book swam before my eyes and I could not find the will to concentrate anymore. We had already been in the library for an hour. I needed a break. "Ugh, George," I whined.

"No."

"Why?" I dropped my head to the table.

"Because."

"That's not an answer."

"Fitzwilliam," he cut a glare at me, making sure I knew I was being annoying to him. "You had your answer. No. It is a complete and valid response."

"You don't even know what I was asking for," I teased.

"Yeah, I do," he focused back onto the book in front of him.

"Oh? You can read minds?"

Turning in his seat to face me completely, he smirked. "You're easy to read, you little pervert."

Oh.

Oh!

I could feel my face bursting into a violent flush. I was very interested in the way this conversation was heading. It was a thrill to be under George's undivided attention. And even more of a thrill to be… acknowledged. "Fuck you," I hissed back, like a brat.

"Not right now," George retorted. "You need to behave, we're in the library for heavens sakes." He turned back around in his seat, trying to smother a pleased grin, knowing full well he was not fooling me. He was into this. As much as I was.

"But," I leaned in close to whisper direct into his ear. Enjoyed the sharp inhale as George could not hide his shiver. "I want you."

"Of course, you do," he teased, though he seemed a little strained. "I'm the best."

"Hmmm, yes you are," I continued. "The best at getting me hard with just looking at me." I noted another shiver and this time, George shifted in his seat, as if he was too big for his breeches. "Best at sucking me off."

"Shit, Fitz," he pulled himself into the table so now his lap was completely hidden. "Stop it."

"Best at…" a hand slammed over my mouth.

"I said, stop." He shoved my face away and took several calming breaths.

"Make me," I teased again.

"Once I can stand up, you're going to regret those words," he threatened.

I grinned.

Then stopped.

Not now. No. Nooooooo! Why must there be people? Ugh!

"Wickham," a group of men dropped into the empty seats around the table and demanded attention.

George turned to them and charmed away. I pulled back, letting the conversation happen before me. Why on Earth would I join in? I did not like these people at all.

Their voices grew louder and people in the library hushed us.

Then we found ourselves leaving, heading towards the courtyard. I followed George, like a lost puppy.

"Want to go into town and have some fun?" one suggested.

There was a general chorus of agreements. Another asked for clarification about what sort of fun.

"Wine and women, of course!"

I frowned. Women?

"Wickham?"

George hesitated a second, not noticeable to anyone else but me, before going forward. "I'm in," he announced as he turned to look over his shoulder. "Fitz?"

No.

No!

I wanted to yell and grab George and haul him away back to our room. Lock the door to keep these… horrible people who wanted to take George for their own pleasure.

To be with someone else… with a woman? It churned my stomach.

"I'm going back to the dorm," I stated.

George grimaced. "Fitz, it's okay."

Was it? I did not think it was.

"Yeah," laughed one of the other boys. "We all had to fumble our way through our first time," they teased. There was a general laugh that followed.

I did not like them. Hated them even. First time? Meeting George's eyes I saw the knowing look there, a twinkle and beginning smirk curling the corner of his lips. We had had been each other's first for everything; kiss, touch, love.

But… did George want to bed a woman?

Did he only go along with me for fun?

Without further words, I turned on my heel and marched off. I heard the teases called out by everyone but George.

*

Hours of waiting in our room. Hoping he would come to his senses and come back to me. And nothing.

I went to bed alone.

Sleep eluded, taunted me. My mind imagined so many things and…

When the door opened and closed, I stayed still. Not wanting to face him yet.

A moment of silence.

"I know you're awake," George said.

I gritted my teeth. "Don't, George."

"We have to talk," he locked the door, the click deafening in the pregnant silence. Even the normal exciting sound of the lock clicking, made me want to vomit.

"Why?" I snarled. "I don't want to hear about…"

"It's necessary," George said over the top.

I surged up in bed and stared at him.

George dumped his jacket onto the end of the other, unused, bed in the room. "Think for a second, Fitz," he stripped. Undoing his loosened cravat, shrugging off his waist coat, and finally tearing the shirt over his head.

That is when I saw them. Hickeys. All over his neck and chest. New ones that overlapped the ones I had given the night before.

"This act puts us above suspicion," George continued. He yanked off his boots and dropped his breeches.

Looking away, not wanting to see where else evidence of another person had been, I snapped. "What are you talking about? What suspicion?"

The sound of water pouring into the basin told me where George was in the room.

"People already think we're too close, even for childhood friends," George explained. "If a rumour starts, even as a joke, they will look at us and could find some sort of evidence of us doing something wrong. Your family would be ruined and we would be wearing matching nooses."

I shuddered, the fear very real and surging in my belly. "That's why…"

"No," I snapped. George was being logical but it did not mean it did not hurt. "We are careful. We are fine. We do not need to do anything with women to prove ourselves to other people." I insisted.

A splash brought my eyes finally round to George. Where he had thrown the wash cloth into the basin and now glared at me in pure frustration. "What part of noose around your pretty neck are you not understanding?!" George jerked a clean shirt from my draw and pulled it on with sharp movements. The linen hit the middle of his thighs and hid the worst of the marks. "Because I do not want that to be how we end up. Ever. I will not let it happen!"

I sulked. "I do not like this."

"I don't either."

That response was so fast. I stared. Did he mean what I wanted him to? That he did not take pleasure from laying with a woman? That I was still the only one he wanted to be with?

Because he was the only one I wanted. Not women. Not even other men. Just him.

George looked exhausted, standing in the middle of the room. Waiting.

I knew he was waiting, waiting for permission to come closer.

It hurt. I ached for it to be the other day when we did not have to be having this argument. When this was not real, and we could pretend the outside world did not exist and could lay in each other's arms.

I lifted the blankets in invitation.

George stumbled over. Crawling into the space and immediately burrowing his face into the crook of my neck. Inhaling deep before releasing some tension on the exhale.

I gave in. My arms came up and gripped George tight. Never wanting to let go.

We settled for a moment.

Then… "Did you… enjoy it?" I was stupid and asked.

Silence.

I swallowed hard, jealousy rearing its ugly head in my chest.

"I disliked it," George admitted, his voice muffled. "Physically, it felt weird. I had to pretend that it was not her."

"Why didn't you stop?"

"Because if I act like a rake, everyone will think I am one." He sighed. "They'll never question me about… preferences," he added.

"But you don't want it." I argued.

"I want to keep you safe," his arms about my waist squeezed. "Always. And this is the only way I can do so."

"You think I don't want to protect you either?" I asked in a panic.

George jerked his head up and wrinkled his nose. "I know you want to keep me safe. But your safe is to lock us away in Pemberley and never leave. That is suspicious."

"No, it is not! It is our home!"

George smiled. "Yeah," he said, soft. "Home."

The mood shifted with that word.

Letting the fight leave my body, I snuggled, pressed a kiss to his temple.

*

It happened often. George, pulled away by his 'friends' to go and have 'fun,' would come back to our room, exhausted and reeking of perfume.

Always before climbing into bed, he scrubbed his skin.

This I did not like. I did not want to share him with anyone. I wanted it to be us.

And he was exhausted. Each encounter left him too tired to want to do anything with me.

Waiting for him to come home left a soured taste in my mouth. Each minute he was not there meant my mind filled in the gaps. It supplied images of women on their knees sucking him down. Faceless women bent over the end of a bed screaming in ecstasy as he screwed them. Or women straddling his lap and impaled on him staring into his eyes.

So, I spent time outside of our room.

I went walking. I went drinking at reputable establishments that did not allow women to enter. And after a long while, I went home.

I stumbled to the bed. George was already knocked out cold, mouth hanging open, and drool pooling on the pillow.

Not caring that I was a full-grown man and could cause a lot of pain, I collapsed on top of his prone body.

Startled awake, George sucked in air and yelped. "Fitz!"

"Hmm," I hummed into his skin, settling so we were chest to chest, my nose under his jaw. "I miss you."

He stiffened underneath. And then softened. "I haven't gone anywhere."

"Not true," I argued. I was not being fair to him at all. But he had chosen this persona, chosen the path of a rake as his armour. I squeezed him tight in aggression.

He shifted in my grasp. "Ease up, Fitz. I'm gonna die if you don't let me breathe."

Aggression took over. I gripped his face hard and turned him to kiss me.

He went still.

My tongue dominated his mouth, flicking in and out, rolling with his. I forced my leg between his thighs and pushed harsh against his growing arousal.

"Hmm, Fitz," he hummed.

I stared down at his flushed face, wet lips parted as he gasped for air. "Let me," I demanded.

He paused. Then nodded. "Yes," and took it, took everything I gave him. It sated the monster inside of me because no woman could do this to him. No woman could find George's sweet spot and make him break.

This George was mine.

Mine.

No-one else's.

*

"Another late night, eh Wickham?" an elbow shoved into his ribs.

A playful smirk was the only response.

Oh yes, it had been a late night, I thought. I had struggled to wait until we had been behind a closed door. Grabbing George and erasing the memory of anyone else touching him.

Kissing him.

Fucking him.

I had bent him over and worshipped his arse, kissing and biting it before reaching for the oil and preparing him.

Dropping his head to the sheets served to lift his hips higher.

He was perfect. I could not wait. I pushed inside slow, drawing it out until I filled him completely, hitting that hidden place for him.

I was fast and sloppy.

Hell, I had only dropped my breeches, I was still wearing my boots and shirt.

Blasted shirt!

It hung too damn low, catching between us as I thrusted into George. Furious that I had to slow the frantic pace, I grabbed the back of the offending material and ripped it off over my head.

George Whined. "Fitz… please… don't stop."

Snatching his shirt up, I bunched it between his shoulder blades and held on, resuming the rhythm from before. "I've got you," I soothed.

Each moan from him fed the insane fire within me. He was like this because of me. These sounds he made were mine!

George threw a hand back.

I dropped my chest to his spine. He threaded his fingers into my hair.

Each jerk of my hips made him gasp and pull harder on my scalp.

Damn it, this was addictive.

I took hold of his dick in my fist and started to move in tandem. This sent him spiralling further into incoherence. Pre cum drooled, helping the glide of movement.

He was close. So close. "Come on, cum for me, my love. Spill it all over the sheets," I hissed into his ear. My hand focused on the head of his cock, right where he liked it. Hot. Sticky.

He screamed.

I slowed to a gentle rock of hips as my hand worked the last few drops from him.

"Good, George," I pressed a kiss to his damp temple. "So good for me."

Straightening up, I ran my palms over his back.

He shivered. "Fitz?"

Then it was back to the same pace as before. Hard and fast. Each one hitting the spot deep inside of him that made him loose control.

He cried out and begged. "No, no, stop, fuck… it's… oh, fuck me. Please. Please," he sobbed.

My fist returned to his dick and continued to over stimulate. As I came, George came again. He tightened on my cock… this was the best.

We collapsed onto the bed. Keeping my weight from crushing my limp lover, I rolled us to the side. But as I started to slip free of him, he tensed and in a panicked voice begged me. "No, don't leave me."

It was so pitiful, it broke my heart.

I rushed to push back into him all the way. "Shh, I'm not going anywhere," I reassured. My arms wrapped tight around him.

His hands came up to grip them.

"I love you," I kissed the back of his neck. "I love you, George."

"Hmm," he responded, sleepy.

I dropped kisses to the nape of his neck. "Tell me."

"What?" he grumbled.

"Tell me you love me." An order.

He sighed and turned his head as best he could to look at me. "You fool."

"Tell me," I demanded.

"I love you," he murmured back. "How can't you know?"

"Our condolences, Mr Darcy."

Do not call me that.

"He will be missed."

Of course, he will be!

"We need to discuss your father's last will and testimony, Mr Darcy."

Stop calling me that!

They said my father passed from a broken heart mere months after my mother. But I will never know, because I was away from home for both of them.

And I was no longer a son.

I was Mr Darcy. A gentleman. Master of Pemberly. Guardian to my baby sister.

Every decision I made would affect more than me from now on. Forever more. A household filled with staff, properties homing tenants and land that had to produce. All of them were my responsibility now.

Father had promised he would show me the necessary workings of Pemberly. Then, as I became more capable, he would pass the day-to-day workings over to my care.

He had broken his promise.

My father was dead.

Georgiana was inconsolable. She was so young. It should not have been like this for her.

I was an adult. In a way, I was luckier than her. I had all my childhood and teens and early twenties, so much of my life, with my parents right there. Always there.

Unfortunately, there would no longer be a mother for her to spend time with. No longer have the security of knowing she was always safe under father's protection. No longer be able to feel their love in a hug or a kiss to the forehead.

As we walked from the church to the graveyard, she had slipped her tiny hand into mine and gripped hard, sobbing.

I squeezed back and tried my best to keep a stiff upper lip.

George walked behind us. There, but not a part of the family. Not by my side.

No, instead I had the absolute privilege of having Lady Catherine by my side. She used her cane to propel herself forward. "It won't be long and you lot will be coming to Rosings for my funeral," she announced.

Cousin looked over her head at me and grimaced.

I rolled my eyes. As if she was anywhere near ready to leave this mortal world and rest.

Her daughter, Anne, coughed into her handkerchief.

"Surely not, Aunt," Cousin pandered. He patted the hand she had on his arm as he escorted her. "You can't leave us yet."

She scoffed. "Young man, I tell you I can feel it in my bones. You too will understand when you have reached my age." And off she went about how she suffered. How she was going to die.

Yet, it was my parents that were now laid to rest side by side.

Lord, I wish she would be quiet.

"Brother?"

I turned to Georgiana.

She sniffled. "Is aunt unwell? Is she…" she trailed off.

I shook my head. Tilting down, so my voice did not carry, I whispered to her alone. "Ignore her. She is just talking."

Georgiana nodded. And her shoulders relaxed. Had she been truly worried that she was going to lose someone else so soon? She need not do so. Lady Catherine was most likely going to outlive all of us through sheer determination.

The minister finished his piece and dirt thrown onto my father's casket. I stared at it, not seeing it, but unable to tear my eyes away. His casket. In the hole in the ground. Father. He was… and next to him… Mother.

A solid hand thumped onto my shoulder, jolting me.

"Fitz," George said soft. "It's time to go."

Oh. I realised that it was over and most had already left. Cousin had guided Aunt away, thank goodness, and it was only Georgiana and George. I jerked a nod.

That hand slipped from my shoulder. George again followed behind. As dictated by the rules of our society.

"Let's go home," I said. And Georgiana bobbed her head in agreeance.

"Anne and I will stay as long as we're needed at Pemberly," Aunt announced as we came closer.

So, you will be in a carriage and heading back to Rosings right now? How convenient. Of course, we were not so lucky. She stayed for days. Anne lurked nearby her side at all times. And Cousin, the coward, left. Went back to his responsibilities. Making me have to deal with our aunt.

I loved her, she was family after all, but she was easier to love when she was several miles and counties away in Rosings.

*

At dinner, I moved to my usual spot. But it was empty of a place; the servants set it at the head of the table... Georgiana stayed in her place. As did George. The others taking up their appropriate spots.

No problem, I redirected my feet and took my place. At the head of the table. Then tried to ignore how… wrong it felt. Like a child playing dress up. I should not be here. Not yet.

And the empty seat opposite… where Mother had sat…

I did not eat.

*

"Ugh!"

My mind was a jumble. Since the lawyer had me sign papers and congratulated me on becoming master of Pemberly, I had spent almost all my time in my father's… *my* office. Reading over every piece of paper and every ledger.

Not that I was also hiding. No, of course not. My aunt did not annoy me that much. I was working and losing my mind at the same time. My curses filled the air.

What use was Latin and philosophy when I needed to know how to balance books? How was I to go around and collect rent from my tenants? I did not even know my father had done that!

"Damn it!" I dug my fingers into my hair and yanked on the roots. This was the most frustrating thing in my life I had ever had to deal with. I knew nothing and had no-one I could turn to for help.

"You look like shit."

My head snapped up at the sound of his voice.

George closed the door behind him, flicking the lock.

I gaped at him. "You have no idea what I have to deal with." I slapped my hand down onto the pages before me and seriously considered sending them over the edge of the desk. Only that would be a mess I would have to clean up. Reorganise it. And no, that was not something I wanted to do. Instead, I slumped back into the chair and groaned.

A humourless chuckle. "I'm sure I don't." He came around the desk and sat on the edge.

When within reach, I placed my hands on him. "I am… I just…" my voice wobbled.

George's eyes shone with unshed tears. "I'm sorry, Fitz."

And with that, we both broke.

We collapsed into each other and cried. My hands dug into the back of his jacket, holding him hostage for my needs only. No, I would not let him go. No. Never again. I had to hold onto him.

Hot tears burned my neck from where he buried his face.

Sobs racked my body. I passed them on to George and he passed them back to me. Over and over. Until the tears ended.

We cleaned our faces with kerchiefs and laughed at how ridiculous we looked. "Silly."

"Shut up," he pinched my ruddy cheek. "You look like you haven't slept at all."

"It feels like it." I inhaled, held it, and released it slow. Yes, the tears had stopped for now. Standing, I moved to the side table with the whiskey. Now was a perfect time for a stiff drink.

I poured two generous glasses that sloshed and clinked in the silence. George went and reclined on the lounge, eyes unfocussed. "Here," I pushed a glass I was offering into his hands.

"Thanks," immediately, he downed half. Hissing afterwards. "Damn. That is the good stuff."

"Obviously. Not in some dirty alehouse anymore," I teased.

He scoffed soft. "Obviously. This is absolute luxury," he countered.

We fell silent for a time.

"He left you a living," I told him, my voice barely over a whisper.

George nodded.

"One problem."

"What?"

I met his eyes as I sipped. "It's for the church."

He snorted.

I joined him.

"Honestly?"

I nodded. "Father thought that you would make an excellent man of the cloth. Had this small parsonage and a good living set aside for you."

"Me?! For the church?" he slumped back into the lounge. "Especially after what we've done together?" he murmured.

I rolled my eyes at him.

"Do you…" he started.

"Do I what?"

"Do you think I should be ordained?" he asked.

Wow. Blinking, I took a moment to consider this. George as a minister… it was laughable. Yes, he was bloody brilliant at charming people. Could hold an audiences' attention with a story. But, George? A minister? Talking about sin when he committed it frequently? Absolving others when he and I were probably never going to be able to admit or be absolved ourselves?

"Jeez," he brought me back to the present. "Didn't realise you had to take that long to think about a simple yes or no." He rose up and moved to refill his glass.

"Do you even want to join the church?"

"I asked first," he fired back.

"You would excel at anything. You could be an amazing minister. But I know you and what you have done and it would be hypocritical for you to be preaching abstinence when you do not. At all. Ever."

George laughed. "Have you ever met a man of the cloth that isn't a hypocrite?"

I shrugged.

We ran into some men of the cloth inside some rather unsavoury establishments. Once or twice. In a night.

"If you want, you can have a lump sum instead of the living," it was the least I could do. Since it made no sense in my mind. Even if my father had believed it would suit him.

He came back and collapsed onto the lounge. This time lying across it, legs kicked over the armrest and head nestled into my lap.

My hand drifted to his hair and started to play with the strands. Twirling locks around my fingers. Scrubbing my fingertips over his scalp.

He hummed.

"I'm scared, George," the admission made.

He looked at me. "Of what, Fitz?"

"Everything. It is too much for me. I do not know what I am doing or who to ask for help. Everyone here is dependent upon me and they all expect me to know what to do and keep things running as before." My hand tightened into a fist in his hair. Wanting it to ground me.

"You'll learn," was all he offered.

That was it.

I frowned as he did not add anything else. "Nothing else?"

"I do not know what else there is, Fitz. I do not know how to run Pemberly. Or what you have to do to keep it going. But this is you. No matter what, you have always learned to do everything.”

As far as encouraging and inspirational, it lacked.

Perhaps this was payback for taking too long to answer before.

Or he really did not know either.

*

Aunt left with Anne. We were very sad to see her go… “I expect to see you at Rosings soon,” she turned her cheek in expectation.

I dropped the kiss there. Did not answer her.

“Safe journey,” Georgiana wished them.

“How safe can one be when travelling as far as we have to,” she said, the footman handing her into the carriage. “But we’ll manage, we always do.”

Anne nodded. She opened her mouth to add something, but her mother spoke over the top of her. “Do not be too proud, Fitzwilliam. All you must do is write to me and I will assist you in all manners.”

“Thank you, Aunt,” I bowed. Sometimes, it was clear she had good intentions.

“Of course,” she continued. “It would be better if you hurried up and married. Pemberly needs a mistress to care for it.”

I grimaced.

*

Sauntering in from a day spent away from Pemberly, probably so he need not have to see my aunt off, George grinned.

"George!" Georgiana raced and leapt into his arms as soon as she saw him.

He laughed, catching her and spinning her around and around. "Georgiana!" He squeezed her tight. Affectionate kisses dropped to her temple. Like a brother would.

She hummed and rested her head on his chest and stayed there.

Had it been any other man, it would have been inappropriate. But this was George. He was like family. And I trusted him. He would never hurt my sister. In fact, if she ever gathered the courage to admit her crush to him, I was positive he would do his best to let her down gently.

Yes, I knew she had a crush. It was hard not to like George. I knew how hard. None of us Darcys were immune to him.

She hung off his arm as we walked to dinner. Along the way, she asked questions. All with her childlike wonder and obliviousness. George humoured her, looking over her head to me in silent communication.

I shrugged and let him suffer this inquisition.

We sat to dine. I turned my focus to the conversation Georgiana was hosting with George. The same way my father had given me space and time to speak, I gave her space and time. Only, she spoke a lot. Rather freely. It would be with us that she would learn to hone her conversational skills. To understand what was appropriate and not.

"What are your plans?" she asked.

George shrugged. Under the table, he had slipped his shoe off and was rubbing at my leg.

"Oh, come now," she insisted. "You have no plans?"

"None," he confirmed.

I removed my shoe and teased him back, smooth arcs of the ball of my foot over his ankle. He enjoyed that. Wriggled his toes to hit the sole of my stockinged foot and tickle, a little.

"But you are educated and can do anything! Can go and be anything," she exclaimed.

"Perhaps," he sipped his wine. "If I had ambition to."

"You don't have ambition to be something?"

George's foot froze.

I shot my sister a warning look.

She completely ignored me, instead mulled aloud over this puzzle. "But what else is there for you to do? Even brother has his work of being master of Pemberly. Do you not want to become a soldier or a sailor and travel and have grand adventures? Or join the clergy? You have a wonderful way of speaking, you would deliver sermons beautifully!"

The food began to sour in my mouth.

George's foot withdrew from mine. "All very honourable pursuits," he commented. But there was an undertone of discomfort.

"I do not understand," she continued blithely. "I know I will grow up and then find a husband and have children and run his house."

That is expected of her… I glanced at George and… worried. The last time I had seen him plaster on that look… oh no. He had agreed to a night out and did not come home until the wee hours of the morning reeking of perfume and sulking.

"A man is meant to achieve things in his life." She added.

"Georgiana," I pushed through clenched teeth.

One look at my face and she realised. "I mean," she stumbled over her words to correct herself. "I'm so sorry."

George gave her an easy smile. "It's fine," he reassured. "I guess I have been so busy with studying that I had not given it much thought. Now, how goes your piano lessons?"

After dinner, we went to the drawing room to listen to her play.

He was all grace and encouraging words. No outward sign of discomfort lingered and this prompted her to talk freely once more. Though, she chose to steer clear of the topic from dinner.

*

"She's growing fast," he remarked when we retreated to the study once more. He poured two glasses of whisky, offering one to me.

I held it, so I had something in my hands. "She's still a child."

"Soon she will not be. She turns fifteen in a few months."

I frowned at that.

He shrugged. "Saying what is happening. She even knows that she wants to be a wife when she is older."

"That won't be for a long while," the whisky burned my throat. "A long, long while." And only once the suitor has proven they are worthy of my sister's hand. I would not allow some fortune hunter to charm his way into her dowry and break her heart.

George remained silent.

"We should go to bed," I suggested.

He finished off his glass and went for another.

"George," I pushed.

"What?"

"Bed."

He shook his head. "The servants will talk."

I sighed. "You can slip out before anyone wakes up," I suggested.

He ignored that offer and slumped into the lounge beside me. "Hmmm," eyes drifted shut.

"What is it?" I tilted my head to rest on the back of the lounge and stared at him.

"Georgiana is right."

"About what?"

"A man should do something with his life," he swirled the liquor in the glass.

"Forget that," I told him.

"Why?"

"Because she is not right. She is a fourteen-year-old child who has no life experience. The only thing anyone expects from her is to marry and have children. Do you want to take life advice from her?"

Surely, he could see that what she said was her exploring her own thoughts and not something serious. I loved her dearly and she was not a silly girl, but she was only talking. Not considering George's feelings or anything when she spoke.

"But that's expected."

"By whom?" I demanded.

He peeled open his eyes and mirrored my pose, head on the back of the lounge, tilted to face me and stared. "Everyone. Everyone expected you to become the next master of Pemberly. Everyone expects Georgiana to marry well. Everyone expects me to do something with my life."

"Since when do we do what is expected?"

He lifted a brow as if to suggest that was a rather stupid question to ask.

Ah yes. George did a lot because it was expected. That was how he ended up covered in love bites from women. How he ended up with so many 'friends.'

The words slipped from my mouth. "Don't do anything rash."

"Rash?"

"Yes. Let me take care of you, George. Stay in Pemberly and I will take care of us here," I reached out and took his hand, rubbing my thumb over his knuckles. "You do not have to do anything you do not want to."

He chuckled. "Your solution is to keep me as your mistress? Install me under the same roof as your family?"

I smirked at him. "Mistress? Why are you demoting yourself, my love?"

He inhaled sharp. Eyes trained on me as he waited. Lips parted. Body tilting ever more and more towards me.

I pushed forward slow, reaching for him. "Stay with me. I will make sure you never want for anything ever again. I will take care of you for the rest of your life. Just… stay." I kissed him. "Please," I whispered the word against his lips.

George pulled back. His eyes searched mine.

I hoped he saw what he needed. Was reassured, to know I meant it from the bottom of my heart. Know I loved him and would always and make sure he was provided for always.

"I love you, Fitz."

"I love you, George."

Then he was on me, pushing me back into the lounge and pulling at my clothes. Tongue burrowing into my mouth. Thigh grinding into my groin, encouraging me to harden. I groaned and helped him to get rid of my clothes and then his. Needed to be as close to him as possible. "Wait," I hissed, grabbing handfuls of hair and pulling him back.

"What?" he asked, breathless. Face flushed, lips kiss-bruised. God, I loved him.

"We should do this in bed."

He rolled his eyes. "Here," he insisted. "Now," a hot stripe licked from ear down neck to collarbone.

I shuddered and gave in easy. Why would I want to stop this to move it? No, he was right, here and now was the best idea. Ever.

Perfect.

And as we cuddled on the lounge afterwards, sated and happy, we shared little kisses and touches. I hummed, content.

He pushed himself up off my chest and looked me in the eye as he spoke. "Give me the lump sum instead of the living."

"Huh?" my mind was not moving very fast. I pushed sweaty bangs from my forehead as I tried to catch up mentally. "Okay."

His jaw clenched and he appeared to have something else to add. Except he nodded and returned his head to under my chin and snuggled. "Thanks."

I rubbed his back.

Worry gnawed away in my gut, like a rat, little teeth chewing at my intestines here and there. George was thinking. He was thinking about his future and was not letting me in to know what he was deciding or to have input.

And it frightened me.

If he had the living, he would be close by. Yes, he would join the church. But he would live nearby. By taking the money… he could go off…

My arms tightened around him. "George… what are you thinking?"

"That you make a terrible pillow," he complained.

"Be serious. You are not going to stay, are you?"

Silence.

Then.

"No."

That hurt. What I had offered… was not enough. I was not enough. My pride was most certainly slighted from that.

What else? What else could I give him to make him happy and have him stay?

We slept separately and, in the morning, George left.

"Cousin!" dressed in his regiment attire, he greeted me with a hearty slap on the back.

"It's good to see you," I grinned at him and teased. "Colonel."

Rolling his eyes, he made a play to catch me in a head-lock, as if we were children and not grown men. Though, no-one in the gentlemen's club paid us any attention. We laughed and went to our table in the back.

"How are things in Pemberly?" he enquired.

I told him the truth about my last few months. "It has been difficult. I do not know why I wasted so much time in university when none of it has helped me run things. But I have been learning and everyone has been patient with me."

He nodded soberly. "It is to be expected. At least your father left a clear legitimate heir. Imagine if there was no-one? How the staff and the tenants would worry about their future!"

My eyes narrowed. "What are you implying, cousin?"

He sipped his drink. "We're getting to that age, Fitz-william."

"And what age is that?"

"Marriage. Babies."

"Ugh," I rubbed at my temples as he chuckled. "Aren't you a confirmed bachelor?"

He slapped the table hard with his palm and let out a booming laugh. "No. Not if the right woman appeared. But," his smile dimmed. "I am only a second son. It is not expected of me to marry well and produce several heirs for my empire."

"Empire?"

His hand flapped in the air to dismiss that tangent. "You have land and need to have an heir."

I wrinkled my nose at that. "You've been at Rosings."

"Aunt is very vocal. Though if I were you, I would do everything in my power to find a wife of my own choosing."

"Ah. Yes." There was that.

Yet, could I marry a woman and do my duty and father a child onto her? I do not know. If only Georgiana had been a younger brother. Then he would inherit if I did not have a son. Unfortunately, she was a sister and the law did not see her claim to the land.

If it were possible, I would marry George in a heartbeat. But that did not do much for the need for an heir, neither of us capable of carrying a child. And that seemed to be the only real purpose for marriage throughout the genteel class.

"However, I have not been to Rosings in a while," cousin continued. "No doubt aunt will be out to hound me to visit soon and reassure her that I have neither died nor forgotten her."

"Then how did you come to this topic for contemplation?"

"George."

"George? As in my George?" Oh! No, not like that! Look over that slip of the tongue and laugh it off!

He did, thank goodness. "Yes. Your George. That very one."

"When did you see him?"

"In passing the other week. You are not in contact?"

I swallowed. "Not since his last visit to Pemberly a month ago. He does not stay long."

"Understandable."

"How?" I demanded.

"Well, he is trying to figure out his life. It is not like he could lounge around Pemberly for the rest of his days. He has to make a living. Be his own man," he said. "I know that."

"Younger son?"

"Yep. George has it worse. He has no family, no inheritance, nothing."

"He has Pemberly," I mumbled, bitter taste in my mouth.

"No, you have Pemberly. That is your responsibility. And unless he wanted to work as a grounds keeper or something, he has to make his own way in the world."

And that was the reason why he felt like he always had to run off; the expectations of everyone else. I gritted my teeth so not to snap at my cousin to shut up. He knew George and I were close, so he understood that I cared for him as if he was family. But he also assumed like everyone else that George was alone in this world. That he had to rely purely upon his own luck and wits.

*

Georgiana's letter soured my evening further when I got back to the London residence.

She was in the care of her governess Mrs Younge, away from home, to help round out her studies and experiences. I had been all too happy to consent. She needed to have some life experiences before fortune hunters pursued her.

The letter was straightforward. She spoke of her lessons and piano recitals and making new acquaintances. All very much as she should.

But it was the mention of George that startled me. *It is so nice to see him, I have missed him terribly,* she wrote.

Why was he there? Why hadn't he told me of a plan to visit her?

When he had been in Pemberly, we had talked, but it lacked substance. He side-stepped any questions about his whereabouts for the last few months. Or where he was going once he left. Though he did accept another cheque from my willing hand.

We were out walking the grounds, exploring the woods we knew all too well. "Wouldn't it be nice to settle down in one spot," he had said.

"A place other than Pemberly?" I had asked.

He hummed. "I don't think any place could compare to this…" turning on his heel, he looked back the way we had come. Back towards the gardens and the house.

I smiled and tried once again to convince him to stay. "Then why leave here?"

He said nothing.

I bumped my shoulder into his, playful.

He bumped back.

Quickly, we had started to roughhouse and laugh. Then I had him pushed against a tree, my hands cupping the back of his head and tilting it so I could kiss him.

He kissed me back, desperate, gripping my coat lapels and drawing me in closer. "Fuck Fitz, I've missed you."

Leaning back, I gasped into his open mouth. "Then stay this time." I pleaded.

What happened next was a distraction, I knew it then. He swapped our positions so my back was to the tree. Dropped to his knees, hands eager to unfasten my breeches.

"Shit," I moaned.

One touch and I was…

I gripped his hair and held on tight as he nuzzled first the crease of my thigh and hip. Inching closer and closer until he lazily flicked his tongue and made contact. There! Right there! He took the head and sucked on it. The hot heat of his mouth. The flicks of his tongue. One hand cupping my bullocks and massaging, the other taking up the length. Stroking it in time with each pull of his mouth.

My hips bucked on their own, trying to go deeper down his throat.

His eyes looked at me from bellow. Holding me there. Making sure I focussed on him only as he dropped his hands and pushed forward. I went down his throat. His nose brushed my stomach.

I came from it.

He swallowed, not allowing any to go to waste, licking the sensitive head as I slumped back into the tree.

I caressed his cheek, wiping away the stray tears that had leaked out. "Sorry, love."

He nuzzled my palm. "Do not be. You can do what you want with me."

Good heavens above. That had been hot.

He stood and helped to rebutton my breeches. Straighten my clothes. Make me presentable once more.

"What about you?" I pressed my palm to his bulge. Wanted that in my mouth.

He pushed me away. "Later." Kissed me, placating.

To say it had been a confusing visit, would be the start of it. He touched me, wanted to give me pleasure, but anytime I tried to reciprocate, he put it off. But later never happened.

And with that cheque… it did feel a lot like I was paying for a prostitute.

Now I was reading about his visit to Georgiana and her gushing about how nice it was to see him. Something did not sit right.

Colonel Fitzwilliam talking about marriage after seeing George. Georgiana blatant in her crush for George in this letter.

But… no. There was no way… He would never…

It was a snap decision to go and visit. But I would not settle down. If my worries were for nothing then I got to see my sister and possibly George. However, if there was something going on... I could alter things before they happened.

Georgiana was so happy to see me. She raced to be in my arms.

And when I saw from whom she had run… I wanted to throw up as we stood in the sitting room of the small townhouse.

She confessed everything immediately. The words love and marriage and happiness, flew out of her mouth like they were true. Then she asked for my consent.

I had to remind myself. She does not know what she is doing, she thinks she is going to marry the man she loves. She is a child. Fifteen. What does she know about love and forever? And what does she know about George?

George was taking advantage of her. There was no other explanation. But why?! He had money. I had given him more. Happily, I would always give him an allowance.

So, why?

I knew he did not desire women and his love for her was fraternal. Wasn't it?

"Georgiana, go and pack your things," I said through clenched teeth.

Her happy face disappeared. But she was smart enough to know this was not the time to argue. She nodded and went to her rooms.

I glared at George before heading to the study.

He followed.

"What the hell, George?!" I exploded once we were in the safety of the private room.

George looked to heaven, as if there would be a divine power to come to his rescue. "It is a rouse. I do not love her."

"But she loves you!" I roared.

George flinched.

"My sister," I continued. "My fifteen-year-old sister!"

"Fitz…"

"She is a child! You have known her since the day she was born!"

"Listen to me…"

"How could you do this?!"

"I'm desperate!"

I narrowed my eyes. "You're desperate?"

"Yes. And if you shut up long enough, I can explain."

"I fucking doubt it," I sneered. But held my tongue, wanting to hear this reasoning for convincing my little sister to elope. It would be so important and moving, I am sure. Ha!

"I do not want to leave you, Fitz. I do not want to have to give you up and have to leave. Georgiana would be the legal connection. And we would be together always. We would live at Pemberley. No one could ever suspect us. It would be perfect."

What… he was serious? I stared in horror at the man I loved and wondered when he had gone mad. When he stopped seeing reason and kept on scrambling to hold on tight. Afraid of something that was only a possibility, not a guaranteed disaster.

"It wouldn't be perfect," I told him, tone dark and leaving no room for argument.

George opened his mouth to protest.

Speaking over the top, I stopped him. "Georgiana is in love with you. She wants you to be her husband and to love and cherish her. This would devastate her if she found out you did not return her affection equally."

"I do love her," he muttered.

"It is not the same," I snapped.

"People get married all the time without love. I do not understand how this is anything different," he looked confused. "I protected us back in Cambridge with my reputation. This is the same thing."

Anger burst, filling me with a hot rage that I moved without thinking. Slamming George to the wall so hard, the painting hanging to the side rattled. "It's my sister!" Pinning George with all my weight, pressing my forearm across his chest, I leant in close to hiss cruel words. "Her happiness is my priority."

George blinked.

And then…

"Are you kidding me?!" He brought his hands up and shoved me back. "After everything I have done for us, and you are prioritising someone else?! She's your sister, whoop-de-doo. I am your lover! Me! I make you happy!"

"No, you do not!"

George reeled back as if slapped.

"Not for a long time, George," I admitted.

"What?!"

"You are obsessed with keeping this appearance up! Making sure that everyone knows that you screw women and acting like it is the only way to protect us. It hurts me, George! It hurts! I hate it!"

Leaning in close so his hot breath seared my face, George snarled. "Do you think I liked it?! Bedding those women made me sick. I hated every second! I did not do it because I liked it! And you would not know because you refused to make the same sacrifice!"

"That's because I'm not scared like you!"

"You should be!" There was a pause. George continued. "There was another couple sentenced to death last week."

I closed my eyes. Yes, I had heard the news. Felt the panic too.

Sodomy had been illegal in England for hundreds of years. Punishable by death. Though, many chose to flee the country if they had the option, never to return to their homes or loved ones again.

Not that the law prevented it from happening. Obviously, there were others like George and I who risked it. And there were those out there who hid it.

"Because you don't think it will happen to us, doesn't mean we're safe." George yanked on his coat and straightened it. Striding across the room to pour a stiff drink from the side board.

That was not why I did not have the same reservation. Many men acted the same as we did without being in love with one another. An arm slung over a shoulder. Leaning in to whisper. Spending every spare moment in each other's company. Being seen at all societal events together.

Men did these things platonically all the time.

And I knew that it was pointless to worry and live in fear. As long as we never did anything explicit in public like kiss, there would never be evidence against us.

It had been over a decade and we had never been caught.

Even in Cambridge, when we were silly and young and had the freedom of sharing a bed for the first time. We had been careful.

I pinched the bridge of my nose and went to slump into the chair behind the desk. "This is too much."

With a clink of glassware, George filled another and brought it to me. "You know I'm right."

I glared at George in response.

I had admitted, that I could see the logic behind George's actions and how the perception would cover the truth. But I did not agree with it.

And I most certainly would never consent to a marriage between George and Georgiana.

My sister.

She would be heartbroken if she found out… and worse, if she knew the relationship that George and I had shared.

Not to mention how I disliked the thought of sharing him with her. This was not a toy I could hand over… this was George. My George.

"What now?" he asked.

I reached for the drink. Tossed it back. The whiskey hit my throat, the burn a welcomed distraction for a moment. "I can't do this anymore."

"Please be specific, Fitz. Because I cannot try to guess what you mean." Exasperation made him snap.

"Us." Was that specific enough?

George panicked. "No. No! Fitz, look I'm sorry. I will not try anything like this again. I will make up some lie about wanting to marry Georgiana for her dowry and have her hate me."

I felt the tears prick the back of my eyes. Shit. I did not want to do this, did not want to end it here like this.

"Please," he stumbled around the desk and cupped my face. "Please do not end it here for us. I'll do anything. Please." He begged, desperate.

I swallowed hard, trying my best not to cry. Looking at George was not helping.

Fuck.

Shit.

Damn it all to hell!

I reached up to hold onto the hands that clung so desperate. Hands I had known all my life. Hands I had been touched by, loved by, hurt by.

"George," my voice broke.

"I love you, you idiot!" and in a fit, he smashed his mouth over mine.

I kissed him back. Then pushed him away. "I want you to never return to Pemberley."

"No," he held on tight.

"We can't keep going like this," I stood from the chair and forced George off of me. "It has to end and you need to leave."

"Why?!" George demanded.

"Because I…" no, not true. I would always love George. Always have less of a heart because I had given it to him. "Because I do not… love you, anymore."

"Liar!"

"Does it matter?!" I snapped back. "I cannot do this. The schemes and performances and now you trying to marry my sister! How am I meant to explain to her and everyone else who knows that you no longer hold an interest in her? But you can stay in Pemberley like it never happened? You made this mess!"

"So now you care about appearances?"

"I never said I did not. I knew that if we were careful, we could live how we wanted without anyone knowing. You were the one who had to make it into a show of who was the bigger whore." I pulled out the cheque book from my pocket. Quick and efficient flicks of my wrist and I filled out a piece of parchment with a healthy sum.

I thrusted it, ink still drying, into George's chest. "Get out."

George scrunched it up, looking ready to throw it into the fire. "You are a bastard, Darcy," he snarled. Shoving the cheque into his coat pocket, he stormed out of the room. Slamming the door so hard it rattled the frames on the wall.

I broke then. Hot, angry tears fell. I doubled over in pain as my heart ripped clean into two pieces.

No no no, what had I done? This was all wrong. That was not how I should have handled that. I had scrawled that cheque without thought. Had said those words without care.

But I had been considering for a while what it would mean if we stopped being Fitz and George. Wondered if it would be a good thing to try and be friends instead of lovers.

My knees gave out from under me and I crashed to the floor. Hidden behind the desk, I leant against it for support.

It was all a mess. I had lost the man I'd spent the entirety of his life loving in seconds.

A tentative knock came from the door.

No!

It clicked open and a timid voice spoke. "Brother?"

I covered my mouth. If I was silent, she would leave and search elsewhere.

"Are you alright?"

I heard her light steps as she entered the room and closed the door.

I wanted to yell at her to get out. But if I snapped, she would be hurt. It was not her fault. It was not even George's fault. It was my own stupidity. I swiped at the trails of tears coating my face and cleared my throat. "Everything is fine, Georgiana. Please leave." She had not even seen me cry when we buried our parents.

Creeping around the desk she found me. "I'm sorry," she dropped down beside me. And as if she was the older of us, she gathered me into her arms with a hush and firm grip.

I took the comfort, hands coming up to grip onto her arm, tears falling.

"I'm sorry," she repeated into my hair.

We never spoke of it ever. But when we were safe in that study, we Darcy siblings showed emotions we normally concealed.

Chapter Six; Bingley's Offer

It was like I had lost my balance. Spinning out of control, nothing to tether me to reality. Nothing to make me want to get up in the morning and live.

No more visits or letters, not that those had been plentiful in those last few months. But this was worse. No contact whatsoever. I had no idea about his whereabouts or with whom he associated.

I wanted to know. Needed to know. Ached to see him again. To hold him. Anything as long as it was him.

Georgiana was under a stricter rule. Though I believed she had learned a lesson and would not conceal from me again.

My cousin was aware of the elopement. Only because he too shared guardianship over Georgiana. It made me feel ashamed, for him to know I had failed in such a way. And that the betrayal had come from someone I had trusted.

My father would be disappointed in me.

"Darcy?"

I looked around the gymnasium and spotted him immediately.

"Bingley."

Fresh from Oxford, he came over and clapped me on the shoulder. "Good god man! It has been years!"

I smiled and nodded. "It has."

We found it rather easy to fall back into our friendship, especially when we went out to drink. "I'm sorry about the loss of your parents," he said.

"I'm sorry about your father," I replied.

Silent, we toasted in memory.

One drink turned to many. Bingley's tongue loosened. Everything came out. I recognised many of those feelings. The grief of losing a parent. Fear of having to fill the position as head of the family. Unease and second guessing.

"I know," I reassured. "I know."

At some point, there may have been tears. My shoulder became water logged. And that was fine. I wanted to be there for my friend.

The next day, while I was coping poorly with the hangover, Bingley called upon me. He did not seem to suffer from the same infliction. Instead, he chuckled and sipped more alcohol from my side board as if the world was fine.

I glared from the lounge. "I hate you."

"Sure, sure," he smothered his laugh into his hand. Before clearing his throat and looking determined. "I have an offer to make you."

I cocked a brow. "Business?"

"No. Actually, this is personal," he fiddled with his nail. "I want you to join me at Netherfield."

"What is Netherfield?"

"It's a rather charming property in the country I have signed the lease for." He started to glow with the excitement. "My sister, Caroline is going to be taking care of the household," he added. "And my other sister and her husband are coming to live with me for a while."

"Sounds like a full house." And not for me. Though I had crossed paths with Bingley's family before, even

Georgiana had met them. I would not say I was comfortable living with them and spending all that time out in the
country…. With no escape.

"It is a very large house, Darcy. Lots of room. Even a
small library," he tried to entice me.

I narrowed my eyes.

"And I would like to have my friend there," he admitted.

Ugh, why did he have to ask so sincerely? I could see
his problem. Being the head of his family with two older
sisters always there and always instructing him. I too
would want my own backup. "Is that the only reason?"

Bingley pondered before speaking. "You look like you
could do with some time away amongst friends."

"What does that mean?" my tone became defensive.

He stumbled over his words to reassure me it was not
malicious. But only started to make sense when I placated
his worries. "You appear to be rather sad, that is all. And
if I could help you by inviting you to have a jolly good time
in the country, then yes, I most certainly make this offer."

"And it has nothing to do with having an excuse to not
always deal with your sisters?" I teased.

He laughed good naturedly. "That does play a small
part."

"Then I would be very honoured to be your guest."

I regretted that decision as soon as we arrived. Miss
Caroline Bingley decided to set her sights upon me.

"Mr Darcy, it is so good to see you again," she purred.

I swallowed down any sort of unsavoury response. Fear, panic, disgust. Instead greeted her and thanked her for the generosity of having me stay with them.

Her hand fluttered to her chest. "We are so grateful to have the pleasure of your company, Mr Darcy. Don't you agree, sister?" She looked over to Mrs Hurst.

She smiled back. "I most certainly do, sister. So grateful for your company, Mr Darcy."

Now I had to dodge whatever plan these two were concocting in their heads. I would not be captured easily, madams, so please do not bother trying.

Bingley swooped into the rescue. "Come with me and I'll show you around." Hastening my steps, I followed him out.

Netherfield was a beautiful estate. "You've made a good choice," I told him. We had explored the house quick before heading straight for the stables. From there we rode out over rolling green pastures and through several wooded areas.

"I'm glad you approve."

"I have a feeling we'll be out here a lot," I commented.

He laughed. "Probably."

*

"I am here to welcome you to the area," Mr Bennet shook Bingley's hand first, then mine.

"It is very kind of you, sir," Bingley said.

"And I should also warn you," Mr Bennet added. "That I have five daughters, and a very silly wife."

Do not react. Do not react. Do not react. It did take all the good breeding within me to not react to such a comment. What kind of gentleman told complete strangers such a thing?

Then again, Sir Lucas the next day came by to do the very same thing and chatted away. Perhaps it was a requirement for living in the area that you do not act with proper decorum. There was nothing wrong with whom we met. They just seemed to be rather a little too forthcoming with their opinions.

"And you must attend the ball, Mr Bingley," Sir Lucas pressed. "It is at the assembly halls in Merriton, and there will be many who would love to make your acquaintance. And yours too, Mr Darcy."

I nodded in acknowledgement.

"We are looking forward to it, Right Darcy?" Bingley tried his best to include me.

Are we? "Certainly," I lied through my teeth. What else could one say? The truth would be offensive. We had only been in the area a week and in no way would I try to sabotage my friend's position amongst his neighbours.

"Jolly good," Sir Lucas clapped his hands together. "Capital!"

The ball… dear God. Someone please set fire to the establishment so I can escape the hellscape that is a hall filled with strangers.

*

"Bingley," I tried to catch his attention. But unfortunately, these new acquaintances were all clamouring over each other to be introduced to him.

Sir Lucas made the introduction for Mrs Bennet and several of her offspring. All their names jumbled in my head and they were all just Miss Bennet to me.

Bingley seemed to be very interested in paying them all attention. Once more, the people-pleaser in him reared its head and that was the last I would see of him for the evening. He danced. A lot.

I hung close to the wall and only took to the floor when Miss Bingley or Mrs Hurst so desired a dance. The sisters seemed rather pleased with this. A handful of rather nasty comments from Miss Bingley comparing this assembly hall to London's, was the last straw for me. I did not take them to the floor again.

I went to find air. Surely there was a balcony or some place to slip off to and not be surrounded by people.

"Darcy!"

Finally, familiarity. I turned as Bingley approached, the biggest grin ever on his face.

"I must have you dance! I cannot stand seeing you mope around like this."

My eyes started to roll.

"I must," he insisted. "There are a number of uncommonly pretty girls here. You should ask one."

Oh, that is how he wanted to play this? "Bingley, you're dancing with the only pretty girl of note." Which one was it again?

"Miss Bennet," he grinned. "She is beautiful, isn't she?"

"Rather so," it was hard to deny that fact. However, I was not completely sure about which Miss Bennet girl he was talking about? The one with golden hair or the darker one? Both were objectively pretty. Though, neither inspired much inside of me to desire interacting with them.

"Look over there," Bingley whisper shouted into my ear.

I followed his non-discreet gesture and spied the dark-haired Bennet girl by the wall.

"That is one of her sisters. She is also very pretty looking."

Ah, so he was talking of the blonde before.

Bingley continued to prod and needle me. Insisting that I needed to pay this young lady some sort of special attention because… she was pretty?

"She is… tolerable," I admitted to him. "But not enough to tempt me. Look, Bingley, you are wasting your time on me. Go and enjoy the smiles of your partner and leave me be."

He shrugged. "I tried."

All a sudden, the dark-haired Miss Bennet glided by us, head held high. My gaze tracked her to the other side of the ball room to another young miss. There, she looked over to us, and spoke to her friend.

Ah.

A hot burning flush of shame flooded my face. She must have heard my comment and was now broadcasting it.

I was doing a fine job of alienating myself with these people.

Mr Darcy is too proud. Thinks he is better than everyone just because he has ten thousand a year. So rude.

And…

Mr Bingley has five thousand a year! He is a perfect gentleman! Five thousand a year! And he pays my Jane special attention, as he should. Five thousand a year!

It made me rather glad that I was an outcast to them. No need to have to defend myself from mamas and their bride-to-be daughters.

The only downside was that Bingley enjoyed the social aspects of the area. Dinners, dances, afternoon tea. So, for me to enjoy his company and his hospitality, I needed to attend.

"I'm inviting Miss Bennet to dinner," Miss Bingley announced over breakfast.

Bingley started to choke on his mouthful. "But…" he spluttered.

"Oh, I know you have plans for this evening already. This is for Louisa and I to get to know her better," she shared an evil smirk with her sister.

Bingley wanted to cancel dinning elsewhere and to stay. But at his sister's urging, he conceded. We went out. He was distracted the entire time. And then he called it an early evening.

"She will be gone," I told him. "We could stay longer." Me? Encouraging socialising with people outside?

Bingley all but ran to mount his horse when the stable hand brought it round. "Maybe. Or maybe I will be able to see her before she does."

I rolled my eyes. Silly man was falling quick for this girl.

The utter joy on his face when we arrived home and Miss Bennet was still there. But then… "Ill?" he repeated the word.

Miss Bingley nodded. "Very ill. Miss Bennet rode over here in the rain. No carriage!"

Mrs Hurst nodded. "It is shocking. How could her family treat her like that? Poor thing."

"We called for the doctor and he says she needs bed rest," Miss Bingley added. "She is in one of the guest rooms now, for the night."

Bingley nodded. "She has to stay then."

"Pardon?" Miss Bingley questioned. "I mean, yes, for tonight."

"No," Bingley objected. "Until she is completely well."

His sisters stared at him. I too, stared at him.

"That could be several days, brother. Even a week," Mrs Hurst informed him.

"And she will be cared for here," he insisted.

*

With Miss Jane Bennet under his roof, meant another Bennet had to come to be by her side.

Miss Elizabeth Bennet. Dark hair, cheeks rosy from her walk, and skirt hem dirtied. She had immediately asked to be shown to her sister.

Bingley came down from visiting the two girls upstairs. "I've asked Miss Elizabeth to stay, also."

"Charles!" Miss Bingley cried out. "Are you planning on moving the entire Bennet household into our own?"

"Caroline," he sighed.

"No. This is getting to be too much."

Mrs Hurst chimed in. "I must agree with our sister, brother. What if the other sisters come and expect you to let them stay? What if their mother comes?" both ladies burst into snickers.

"I would be very much obliged to be a good neighbour to them," he tried to defend. "And you two should be ashamed for being so mean."

"Oh, Charles," Miss Bingley patronized. "We mean no harm."

Lies.

"Darcy," Bingley started.

I nodded. "We should go for that ride."

"Again?" Miss Bingley complained. "You two spend a lot of time outside of this household. Leaving us poor women alone to fend for ourselves."

"We'll be back for supper," I supplied before leading Bingley out of the room.

I was missing Pemberly… or rather the peace of it. No guests traipsing through it. No match makers. No bullies. But if I was to go home… would it be peaceful or a constant reminder that a certain someone would never be there again?

*

After dinner, we moved to do our separate things in the sitting room. Mr Hurst dozed on the lounge. Bingley played cards with his sister Mrs Hurst. Caroline wandered aimlessly. Miss Elizabeth read. And I attended to letters I needed to write.

I could feel Miss Bingley lurking over my shoulder. "You write uncommonly fast, Mr Darcy."

"You are mistaken," I replied as I dipped the quill again. "This is how I normally write."

She started to wander away, thank goodness, but still called out to me so everyone heard. "No doubt a very important letter of business."

"Actually, I am writing to my sister."

"Oh Georgiana!" she exclaimed. "Do tell her I miss her terribly."

"I already have. I will not again." It irked me, the way she acted as if she was friendly with my sister. As if they were good friends. If she had been a good friend to Georgiana then would she not write to her and share a private correspondence?

My focus went back to my letter.

Recounting the last couple of days for Georgiana's amusement. Knowing she would laugh at my expense for being so uncomfortable at a public gathering. But also be so jealous of it. It would be all too soon for her to be old enough to attend dances and balls and I would have to escort her.

Unless I made our cousin responsible for that. That was not such a terrible proposition.

I also added in a few lines about the guests staying with us. *Miss Jane is restricted to her bed, thus I do not have much to say about her. But her sister Miss Elizabeth, who stays to keep her sister company, has been sociable. She is…* queer? I need to change that word choice. Instead, I wrote; *She smiles a lot. In a way that is not because she is happy or wants to set others at ease. Rather because she finds everyone around her amusing and is laughing at them. I cannot confirm if she is malicious in her humorous words to others, but so few react as if they realise she is teasing them. Furthermore, I cannot speak of the woman, I have barely exchanged words with her. This is only what I have observed in passing.*

"Has she grown any taller since the spring? Is she as tall as I am?" Miss Bingley continued.

"Georgiana is about," I paused for a second to consider the appropriate comparison. "Miss Elizabeth's stature or a little taller."

Miss Bingley made an odd little hum. "How I long to see her again. And to hear her performance on the pianoforte once more! How is she with her French? It would be so nice to practice with her in the language."

"Very well," I responded boringly.

"It is astonishing," Bingley announced.

"What is, Charles?" Miss Bingley snapped.

"That you ladies are all so accomplished. You draw, speak other languages, embroider, dance," he said, excited. "Do you not agree, Darcy?"

"Hardly so," was that all that one needed to be considered accomplished? "I believe I only know half a dozen ladies with whom I can call accomplished." Yes, only six, I calculated.

"Yes," Miss Bingley started to list off qualities as if she was an expert. "She must be able to paint, play music, speak several languages. And have something… in her sense of presence," she finished enigmatically.

I did not add to this. But my eyes rolled heavenwards and a sigh started to escape me. When will this end?

"I am amazed," Miss Elizabeth spoke.

My attention went to her, this queer woman. "Of?"

"Of you only knowing six women with such accomplishments. I am amazed you know any at all."

"Are you so severe on your sex?" I fired back, not pausing for a moment.

"Hardly. But I have never met such a woman before," she argued with me. "She would be such a creature to see."

Huh.

What an unusual thing. We stared at one another, her waiting for me to make another comeback in our little banter, and me… a little baffled. Had I not written to my sister thinking Miss Elizabeth was nothing but a woman weaponizing her sarcastic words? A pretty smile? Where had this quick wit come from? And… defiance?

"I must insist, Miss Elizabeth," Miss Bingley interrupted. "That you take a turn about the room with me. It is so refreshing to do after one has been in the same seated position for so long."

The two ladies stood and began to stroll about as if this was a garden and not a sitting room.

"Will you not join us, Mr Darcy?" Miss Bingley asked.

"I will not," I answered.

"And why is that?"

"Because," I do not want to. "I would be in the way."

Miss Bingley laughed coquettishly. "Whatever could he mean, Miss Elizabeth?"

"It would be best if we do not ask," she responded.

"No, I shall ask. What do you mean, Mr Darcy?"

They passed before my small writing table, eyes upon me. With a sigh, I answered. "Either you two ladies have secrets to discuss amongst yourselves. Or you are both aware that your figures are more visible when you are moving. If the first I will be in the way. If the latter, I can admire from afar." Or more likely, not look at all.

"Oh!" Miss Bingley gasped. "Scandalous!"

Mrs Hurst laughed from the other side of the room.

"How do you propose we punish him? Hmm? Miss Elizabeth?"

A hint of a tease tinged her next words. "Simple. We laugh at him."

"Laugh at Mr Darcy?" Miss Bingley scoffed. "Impossible."

Miss Elizabeth stopped her stroll about the room right in front of me. "Are you without fault, Mr Darcy? So much so there is nothing for us to laugh at."

"I am not, Miss Elizabeth. I have my faults." Don't we all?

"And what would one be?" she prodded.

The words slipped from my mouth easy. Like she was someone I could speak freely with. I liked talking to her. Arguing. The banter was amusing. It was similar, yet different, to another person's. "I do not forgive. Once my good opinion of a person has been lost, it is gone."

Her teasing smile softened. "Oh dear. I cannot laugh at that."

A moment passed. Quiet. Intimate. Between the two of us.

But we had witnesses. Miss Bingley interrupted *again* and directed our attention elsewhere. Miss Elizabeth moved back to her seat and I to my letter.

Or attempted to.

That had been enjoyable. I wanted to engage her in more of that sort of banter that flowed. Though, I should do my best to avoid her instead. I believe she still had not forgiven me for slighting her pride before. Everything she said now was either her teasing in retribution or gathering ammunition to feed the gossip.

*

"Oh my," Mrs Bennet sank to the settee with the rest of her daughters. "What a charming home you have, Mr Bingley!"

"Thank yo-" Bingley began.

"It is so kind of you to take care of my Jane the way you have. And she is much better off here than back at Longbourne."

Bingley opened his mouth. Then shut it. Opened. Shut. Over and over Bingley attempted to try to respond. Each time ignored. Over ridden. "Oh, and you sir, are the best kind of gentleman!" she praised him once more.

Bingley nodded and murmured his thanks. Uncomfortable.

When would this all end? After she'd praised him so much he was nominated for sainthood, and for what? All because he was a young gentleman with a fortune? Good grief.

"Of course," her tone soured, she cut her eyes to my direction. "Not everyone knows how to behave like a gentleman," she said, pointed. "Some are too proud to help their neighbours."

Bingley opened his mouth and then snapped it shut. His eyes begged in apology to me.

I struggled not to allow mine to roll. Tiresome woman. Ignorant woman! It stung. Yet again, there was the reminder. I was an outsider and lacked in the qualities that would make me valuable to this neighbourhood.

"Mr Bingley."

"Yes, Miss Lydia?" He latched onto anything that may alter the course of the conversation.

"You should host a ball at Netherfield," she said. "It would be the toast of the neighbourhood."

Her mother and one of her other sisters agreed that this was an excellent idea. None of them seemed to find it rude or imposing to make another person do their bidding.

Miss Elizabeth looked vexed. "Mr Bingley, you do not have to do that. My sister is being…" she trailed off.

But Bingley agreed with Miss Lydia. "I think that is a wonderful idea. And I would be so honoured to be able to host all my new friends and acquaintances here in my home."

Dear God, the man was of another species.

"Once your sister is well, we shall start planning. And you can even pick the date," he offered good naturedly.

"Isn't that nice, Lydia?" Mrs Bennet raved. "That is exactly how a gentleman should be," she looked at me pointedly, again.

Lord have mercy! This was positively getting out of hand.

*

The following day, I was coming back from a brisk walk when Miss Elizabeth opened the door onto the terrace.

"Miss Bennet," I came to a standstill and inclined my head in a bow.

"Good morning, Mr Darcy." She curtsied before stepping through the doorway. Dressed in a bonnet and coat, it was clear she was heading out. "Are you coming in from a walk, sir?"

Dear God, not small talk! And after we had enjoyable banter two nights before. Was that a fluke? "Yes," then paused. This was when most continued the small talk with another question in return, was it not? "And you're about to take a turn around the garden?"

"The woodlands, actually," she nodded in their direction. "I have a need to stretch my legs and I do believe it's a rather pretty area."

From within, we could hear Miss Bingley and Mrs Hurst cackling.

"And far from the house," I let slip.

She failed to suppress her smile. "That too."

I smiled back at her in acknowledgement of the meaning behind those words we had shared. Then, felt like I had to look away. What was that? What on Earth was that? Why was I feeling… uneasy around her? A tingle of a flush crept over my cheeks.

Oh, come on man!

I forced my eyes back to her face. There! Nothing to worry… *oh*. She wore her usual smile, an ever-present tilt of her lips. As if life and those characters apart of it were so amusing to her.

But I thought her smile was… pretty.

Ugh, what is wrong with me? Why was that smile getting under my skin so much? And why on Earth was I opening my mouth with the intention of asking to accompany her on her walk? What?! No!

As I half formed the first words of my question, we were, luckily, interrupted.

"Darcy!" and then, "oh, Miss Elizabeth! My apologies. I did not see you there at first." Bingley came up from behind me.

Bows and curtseys exchanged again.

I sighed. Pleased to not have allowed my foolish self to engage my time further to this woman. And disappointed to have been thwarted. Did I want to spend more time with her? Converse longer?

"How is your sister this morning?" Bingley enquired.

"Doing better, thank you."

"Is she well enough for," he cleared his throat. "A visit? This afternoon? If I am not intruding upon you both."

Miss Elizabeth grinned. "Of course, you are not intruding! And yes, she would be well enough for it. I believe, she would also like that very much." She encouraged him.

"Excellent!" Bingley looked like he could have floated off with the way he bounced on his toes. He looked over to me. Then back to Miss Bennet. Back to me. "Oh, did I interrupt you both going for a walk?"

"No," burst from Miss Elizabeth.

That was fast. No? Was the thought that horrifying to her? Fine. I responded smooth for my own action. "I was coming back."

"And I am going out for mine," she added. Her eyes flicked up to me. Assessing. What was she looking for?

"Ah," something twinkled in Bingley's gaze. Like he had something to say but was enjoying hoarding it to himself instead.

We parted. As I watched her stroll away, I swallowed hard, but still felt like something was stuck there. Perhaps the words offering my company were trapped. Not that… Wait. Why was I… no. Impossible! Did I find a woman attractive?! And not just any; Miss Elizabeth Bennet? When… how…

"Darcy," Bingley shook my shoulder to jolt me. "You're staring at her." He sounded smug.

I ignored him and turned sharp on my heel, storming into the house, as his chuckles followed after me.

*

Thankfully, Miss Jane Bennet's health improved and she was able to leave and return to her own home. Mr Bingley looked devastated at this news. Like a kicked puppy. He tried his best to tell her that he was sad she was leaving. But pleased she was healthy once more, which all came out rather awkward. He was like his teenage self once more, stumbling over his tongue.

Miss Bennet reassured him she understood. Thanked him for his kindness towards her and her sister.

"The pleasure was all mine… I mean." He started to dig himself another hole.

It would be amusing if it was not so painful to watch him display his heart so obvious to this woman. And it would be sweet if she showed the same amount of interest back. Could her smiles be that encouraging to Bingley?

He handed her into the carriage.

Miss Elizabeth curtseyed to myself and Mr Bingley.

I handed her into the carriage. Her tiny hand fitted strangely well into my grasp. Warm. Soft. She squeezed and then let go. "Thank you," she murmured, polite.

I nodded and stepped back. Hmm, that was… right. That was confusing. I had liked that… There is something wrong with my head if I enjoyed a second of hand holding with a woman. Please, take me out back and end my agony before I made a fool of myself.

They drove off and Bingley sighed like a love sick teen. "I wish she didn't have to leave."

"You could have poisoned her food," I offered.

"What?!"

"Then she would have been too ill to leave. Stayed longer."

"Oh… that…"

"No," I laughed. "That was a terrible joke to make. Sorry."

Bingley and I walked back to the house. "Perhaps…"

"No, man," I laughed more. "Think of it like this, if she is healthy, then she can attend balls once more and you can dance with her again."

He brightened at that. "I can't wait for the next dance at the assembly halls."

"Hmm," I hummed, neutral.

He cut a narrowed glare at me as we crossed the threshold and entered the foyer. "Don't think I didn't notice the way you and Miss Elizabeth were making eyes at each other."

"What?" I was genuinely confused. Eyes at each other? Of course, we looked at one another, that was how eyes worked. And one had to look at the person they were speaking to. That was just polite.

"Oh, come on, Darcy. You two were flirting!"

"Hardly!" What was he on about?! I did not flirt!

He batted his lashes and put on an airy girly voice. "Oh Mr Darcy!"

I shoved him away. "Stop! We were nothing like that!"

"You are right," he agreed. "You were more like brooding and staring at her. Only coming to life when you entered some sort of verbal combat with the woman."

This time I reached out to grab at the man.

He ducked. And bounced on the balls of his feet, easy. "What? Too true?"

Yes, but… "No," I reached for him again.

But before we could continue, he held up his hand. "Seriously, Darcy."

"Seriously what, Bingley?" I jerked on the hem of my waistcoat and straightened it. "Are you afraid to fight me?"

He laughed. "Terrified."

We dissolved into chuckles.

"But seriously. Miss Elizabeth is a very amiable woman. She would make a good match." He clasped his hands behind his back. As if he was trying to look more dignified with his messed-up hair and rosy cheeks.

"As amiable as she might be, she is far from interested in my advances." And I was… I mean, did I not have a different preference? She was a woman. Or did that not matter to me… damn it! Not like she was interested in me at all! I am positive of that! Bingley is a love sick fool looking for any romance to obsess over, even when it clearly was not there… or was it?

"Turned you down already?" he dropped any façade and did appear to be in genuine shock.

"I have not made any advances," I swiped at his shoulder in play. "But it is clear I am not going to win any young lady's heart in this part of the country. Especially not with the 'perfect gentleman' Mr Bingley around."

"You need to try to be more likable," he encouraged.

I gagged. "Why? For people who are only kind and polite when they see you have some value? They are not worth my time."

That sobered him. "I will admit, there are some people who are like that."

"Some?"

"A lot," he sighed heavy. "But you attract more with honey than vinegar."

"But I prefer vinegar."

"Of course, you do." He rolled his eyes.

"What about you and Miss Jane Bennet?" I tried to side track him.

"She is perfect," he exclaimed.

Hardly. "Is she interested in your advances, though?"

Bingley looked at me confused. "What do you mean?"

"Is she interested in you? For you. And not because her mother is throwing her at your 'five thousand a year.'" I threw my tone high, similar to how he had done so previously, but added more nasal to it for effect.

He opened his mouth. Closed it. Opened again.

It was my duty to look out for the best interests of my friend. "Perhaps, she will be able to show her appreciation of your kindness and her interest in your advances, now that she is no longer restricted bed rest."

"Yes," he perked up at that prospect.

Because it was fun, I jabbed at his exposed flank. He batted me away and we stumbled into the sitting room.

Caroline Bingley looked up from her needle work and complained. "Are you gentlemen or are you children? Charles! Mr Darcy!"

I made sure to be the bigger man and straightened upright, giving her a bow. "Apologies." Though my hand went out and poked and jabbed at Bingley's weak spots.

He howled in agony. "Cheater!"

I gave him a stern look. "Behave!"

He grinned and threw his arm over my shoulder, looping it tight around my neck and started to drag me out of the room. "I will take him outside right now, sister. Do not you worry."

I laughed as I struggled to break free.

He only tightened his hold. "Now, now, be a man, Darcy. Take your punishments."

Chapter Eight; Unexpected Reunion Extended Version

An innocuous beginning for that day. "Darcy," Bingley tossed his head in the direction of the door. "I am going to call upon the Bennet family. Would you like to join me?"

Or would I like to sit with your sisters and endure their torture as I wait? Ha! "Certainly," I was quick to follow him out the door. We both ignored the disgruntle complaints of his sisters that followed in our wake.

We started the ride over. It was a lovely day to be out, sun warm on the skin, few people on the roads to pass by. Bingley chatted away about this and that. And I was happy to listen and made the occasional remark when I had something to share.

It was pleasant.

Everything was fine as we entered the village. Everything was fine as we spotted the Bennet girls. Bingley excitedly pulled ahead and called out a greeting. Everything was fine as officers dressed in red uniforms turned with the girls.

Then nothing was fine.

His eyes widened in shock. I gaped back at him.

"This is Mr Wickham, we've just made his acquaintance," one of the Bennet girls gushed in introduction.

My heart stopped.

George.

George.

George!

No. I cannot go through this again.

That bastard then had the audacity to smirk and give me a nod of acknowledgement. As if he was not affected by any of this. As if I were a mere acquaintance. Not someone who had loved him with every fibre of my being and offered him every luxury if he had just stayed by my side.

Loved? Or…

Oh shit.

Oh Hell.

No!

Was I stupid enough to still be in love with George?!

"You should invite him to your ball, Mr Bingley," a sickly-sweet voice announced. "You should invite all the officers!"

"Lydia!" someone else snapped in reprimand.

I ran.

When Bingley caught up to me, I had broken every gentleman's protocol and showed weakness in the open. I realised that I needed to leave Netherfield. No-one would care, most would be glad to be rid of me.

Then I would not have to watch.

But George… I wanted to try and talk to him. I wanted to hear his voice. Why was I being such a fool?!

"Sorry."

"Do not be. But, why?" Bingley asked.

I could not meet his eyes at all. "I didn't think I'd ever see him again."

"Who? That Wickham chap? He did look rather familiar. Who is he?"

Who is Wickham?

Who is George?

I swallowed and chose my words carefully. No matter what I said, it had to be a lie. I could never admit that George had been my beloved, that I wanted to spend the rest of my life with him by my side, always. Perhaps even share the same space in the Darcy family plot.

God, I was nauseating.

"George Whickham is not to be trusted," I admitted. "He and I were childhood friends. We grew up together at Pemberly. You probably remember seeing him at boarding school."

Bingley furrowed his brow as he tried to recall our school days.

"We started to go our separate ways back then." Only to reconcile and start an inappropriate relationship behind closed doors. But that is unimportant right now. "It was not until after my father died that Ge… Whickham, betrayed my trust. He hurt my family."

So please do not be friends with him. Do not invite him to Netherfield. And do not pry any further!

Bingley's jaw tightened. "Then he is no friend of mine," he declared.

I do not deserve such a loyal friend. But I am grateful to have him, nonetheless. We returned to Netherfield. Bingley silent along the way.

*

Avoiding was easy when the one you wanted to avoid was avoiding you too.

We did not attend the same social events. However, everyone was talking about him. He was charming. Intelligent. Charismatic.

Many ladies began to declare their desire to be his wife.

"I would not be surprised," Mrs Hurst announced to her sister. Though the rest of us in the sitting room were well informed too. "If one of the Bennet girls was to end up as Mrs Wickham."

Miss Bingley shook her head in dismay. "Every time I see someone, they all tell me that he has been calling upon the Bennet family. He is not that attentive to any other group of ladies in the county. I too would not be surprised if he made one of them an offer."

I gritted my teeth and chose to ignore, to instead focus upon the book in my hands. Not that it was working. I was getting as bad as the ladies, hanging onto the gossip being shared.

"Though, I do believe he has his eyes set upon a particular Bennet girl," Miss Bingley said. Dangled the bit of information in the air, as if to bait someone into asking.

Bingley's head shot up from the card game he and Mr Hurst were playing. "Who?" he demanded.

Miss Bingley waved her hand at him. "Do not worry, brother. Not Miss Jane Bennet." Then her eyes slipped over to mine. "But rather, her sister, Miss Elizabeth. They seem to have a special rapport."

Mrs Hurst jumped in to validate the information.

Miss Elizabeth and George? Well…

I was at a complete loss. My book abandoned. And I could only suffer as the ladies continued.

"Caroline," Bingley cut in forcefully. "That's enough talk of Mr Wickham." He shot me a worried look.

"But why, brother? He is the talk of the town," Miss Bingley protested.

"I need some air," I announced, standing and leaving them behind and heading out to the terrace.

It hurt.

No matter what, I could not escape him. And now, gossip about him contained Miss Elizabeth Bennet… which also irked me.

The ball at Netherfield came. Bingley had invited the officers in general, not excluding anyone, at my request. He was going to ensure that George was never cordially invited to Netherfield. Good man. Good friend.

However, I wanted a chance to speak with George. My silly heart had decided that all we needed to do was talk to him, that it would ease something, solve it. It was like an addiction and after a year of nothing, I craved him.

But he never came. There was something that called him away. Or so they said when giving his excuse for absence.

I wandered the crowded space, adrift amongst the bodies and the inane natter. The overly warm air reeked of perfume and soured sweat. Why did people enjoy such a thing? Why had Bingley been so ecstatic in organising and hosting it?

And why was I not able to spy a single person I could be comfortable around? Oh yes, because I am cold and proud and have not allowed a being we have met near me at all. Obviously.

But then… Miss Elizabeth… She stood out to me. Her head held high, slender neck on display. A simple gown that, well, accentuated her figure… ahem. I had not realised how attractive the female form could be.

I swallowed hard. She was a pretty girl, but… she was more than that. More interesting. I felt myself start to move across the room towards her. I wanted to be close, to hear her laugh, speak with her…

I did not expect the words to be what they were from my mouth. "Would you do me the honour of the next dance, Miss Bennet?" I requested.

And she accepted. I had never wanted to dance with anyone else from our acquaintance.

"I love this dance," She commented as we began the movements.

"Indeed," I murmured. It was hard to speak as we moved around other dancers on the floor. Every word could be overheard by them.

"It is your turn to say something Mr Darcy. I've spoken of the dance, you could remake upon the size of the room or the number of couples."

Great, small talk. Remind me again why did I engage her for this dance? "I am obliged. Please advise as to what you would most desire to hear."

"A reply would do for present." She smiled, playful. "Perhaps I may observe that private balls are much more pleasant than public ones." After a turn she added, "From now we may remain silent."

That lasted for ten seconds before I broke it. "Do you make it a habit to talk while dancing?" I queried as we passed each other.

"No. I prefer to be unsocial and taciturn. Makes it so much more enjoyable, do you think?" she teased.

Excuse me?! Outrageous and rude! Not untrue, I do admit, but to bluntly say it so. However, there was something else I wanted to know. It sat heavy on my tongue. I spat it out. "Do you and your sisters often walk to Merriton?"

She blinked in shock. "Yes, we often do. It is a great opportunity to meet new people. In fact, when you and Mr Bingley happened upon us the other day, we had made new acquaintances."

I scoffed. "Mr Wickham is most certainly blessed with happy manners," I replied, cold. "He is sure of making friends. Whether he is capable of keeping them, is less so." Not that most of his friends were worth keeping. From what I had seen over the years, all sorts attached to George and made demands of him. None were ever real. Shallow, more often.

"He has been so unfortunate as to lose your friendship. And I daresay that is an irreversible event." She sniped.

"It is," I snapped out. "Why do you ask?"

"To make out your character, Mr Darcy," her chin lifted in defiance.

"And what have you discovered?" Come on. Tell me what kind of man I am. Why I am someone not worthy.

"Very little. I hear such different accounts of you, it is confusing," she answered.

I had not expected that. But it still was infuriating, to be thought of so meanly by this woman. I forced out through my clenched teeth, "I hope to afford you more clarity in the future."

The dance ended and I led her off the floor, nodded politely, and left her. Stormed off. I needed to cool my head or… I do not know what I would snap back to her in retaliation.

It had been a mistake.

And what was worse… the thought of watching her fall in love with George. That would be a cruel twist of fate for me. The man I loved being the object of affection for the woman I was slowly falling for. Ha!

"Mr Darcy!"

The whole room went silent with the disruption.

I turned to face the person. A rat-like man I had never met before. He bowed deep and began to talk as if he had leave to be so familiar with me.

"And I must assure you that your aunt, the distinguished Lady Catherine de Bourgh, was in perfect health… last week."

Another one of aunt's minions to spy and report back. I barely acknowledged the statement with a nod, before escaping.

The dining hall brimmed with people and the cacophony of chatter. Over the top some particular voices rose. "And that'll throw the other girls into the path of wealthy gentlemen," Mrs Bennet boasted.

"Miss Lydia!" drew attention to the Bennet girl racing through the crowd, giggling and tossing flirty looks back.

God awful singing and piano playing from yet another Bennet girl.

Did this family completely lack propriety?!

Miss Bingley shared a disgusted look with me at such displays. And I found I could not disagree with her on this. When the piano became free, Mrs Hurst slid into position. She started a perfect performance.

Bingley you fool.

I grabbed a goblet off a tray.

This would become your family if you continue to pursue Miss Jane Bennet. And by living so close... there would be no escape of them. They would invade Netherfield. And Bingley, you are too good natured and eager to please, you would never complain or send them home.

Then again. Watching Miss Jane Bennet interact with Bingley was odd. She did not look like the type of person who wanted the attention of Bingley. Not leaning in to whisper. Touching him in a way that was still socially acceptable yet intimate. Being flirty with her smiles. None of that.

She sat back with proper posture and... nothing.

Was he wasting his time and effort?

Was the mother pushing her because of Bingley's position? She had admitted more than that to all that could hear. She was ecstatic at the prospect of someone of Bingley's status marrying her pretty Jane.

Was the girl being coerced?

The ball came to an end in the wee hours of the morning. Bennet family being the last to leave.

"Darcy," Bingley called out to me as I started to stumble up the stairs.

"Yes?"

He smiled, sleepy. Cheeks flushed from the excitement and a little too much drink. "Tonight was a good night."

I smiled back at him. He did not deserve to have his heart broken. Or life completely ruined by a woman who did not appear to be as in love with him as he was with her. He did not deserve to have that family as in-laws. They would walk all over him and take whatever they so desired.

"It was," I agreed. "Goodnight, Bingley."

"Night, Darcy!"

When we were all awake and capable of thoughts again, I sought out Miss Bingley and Mrs Hurst. As careful as I could, I voiced my concerns.

They both sighed in relief. "We were worried that no-one else would see how unsuitable the match was." Mrs Hurst admitted.

"If I might be so bold to suggest a solution," I started.

The ladies waited for me to speak.

"Quitting Netherfield. Placing physical distance between your brother and Miss Bennet would help to sever the ties. Allow Bingley to see clearly."

They both agreed. Though they moaned about losing what they had gained from living in the neighbourhood. "But for Charles," Miss Bingley said. "We would do anything for him."

"Yes," Mrs Hurst agreed.

Excellent.

Knowing Bingley, he would struggle to stand up to his sisters and advocate for his own desires. And true to my assumptions, he did struggle.

"But, Louisa," he tried to butt in.

"No, Charles. She is far from suitable for you. And," her eyes flicked to me. "Mr Darcy agrees."

That brought gravity to the argument. Bingley looked to me in utter shock. "Darcy, is this true?"

I paced forward. "I am afraid so, friend. I do not want it to be, but I cannot disagree with your sisters. You are in love with Miss Bennet and have been very clear in your attentions towards her."

Bingley blushed like a school boy caught.

"However, Miss Bennet acts indifferent to you. I had hoped that she would warm up and be more receptive once she was over her illness, but that has not been the case." Not even a flirty look toward Bingley had been detected.

And he deserved better than that. He deserved someone who would leave him in no doubt as to how they felt about him.

This was a kind act. "We should leave Netherfield and go to London for a period," I suggested.

"Leave?"

"Leave. Time apart will give you a chance to know if she is in love with you. Or if you have been deluding yourself into thinking this was love. Isn't it better to reflect now than to rush and make a mistake that neither of you can escape later?"

There was the poison. I had poured it into his cup before his very eyes. All he had to do now was drink it and let whatever he was feeling die.

Bingley would find love again. Because he was a good person. It would be easy for him. And it would be the kind of love he deserved.

"I did not know," he whispered. "Did not realise."

"Time apart will give you clarity," I murmured.

"Okay," Bingley relented. He slumped in his chair and dropped his forehead into his hand. "We'll leave Netherfield… and go to town."

"A wise choice, brother."

I am sorry, Bingley. I truly am.

*

We packed.

Servants cleaned, placed cloths over the furniture and closed shutters.

Goodbye was said via letters to certain people. Miss Bingley enjoyed penning the letter informing Miss Bennet. It was clear as she grinned and read the words aloud to her sister for approval.

I overheard from the doorway.

Miss Bennet was saved too, from having sisters-in-law such as those.

We loaded into carriages bound for town. Bingley sat in silence. Mr Hurst slept most of the way. The sisters prattled nonstop; who should be in town, what balls they may still make, if there would be anything worth seeing at the theatre.

It was insufferable.

Once we had made it to London, I took Bingley out. It was only proper to see that he numbed his initial pain with copious amounts of alcohol. After too many, he slumped into my arms and began to cry.

"She was perfect, Darcy"

"She was a woman, Bingley," I reminded him. "They all have flaws."

"Not her. Lord, not her."

So as to not disturb his household, I directed the carriage to my residence in town. The butler knew exactly what to do. Took Bingley, manhandling him as if he was a child and not a full-grown adult. I half expected him to nestle the man into his arms like a babe and carry him upstairs to the guest room. I went to the master bedroom… which still felt so odd to sleep in. Another reminder of how things changed.

I collapsed onto the bed and wondered like I had done numerous times of late; what was he doing? Who was he with?

Another intruder joined George.

Miss Elizabeth Bennet. Every day I found myself thinking of her more often. It was confusing.

Why was love for me so slow to grow and impossible for me to show? And so selective. I did not choose George nor Elizabeth. Fate or some other divine power with too much of a sense of humour had done so. And then watched on and laughed as I struggled with both of them. And failed.

"No," I commanded. "I will not let this control me. I will not."

Surging up and off of the bed, I went about the necessities of getting ready for sleep. Stripped down to my shirt and crawled beneath the covers.

*

"I am so sorry, Darcy," Bingley apologised before breakfast.

I paid it no real attention. "Good man, why would you apologise for something that I caused?"

"Because I must've been an arse to you," he took the chair and started to reach for toast.

"And?"

"And I'm sorry for it."

I huffed a sigh and fixed him with a stare. "You are heartbroken. You are mourning. You have seen me in the same state and taken care of me. This is what friends do."

He gave a sad smile before nodding. The last we would speak on the topic for a long time.

*

"Please, come and sit with me as you wait for Charles," Miss Bingley pleaded.

"Is anything the matter?" I strode into the sitting room after her. Unnerved.

Miss Bingley sighed as she sank to the lounge and folded her hands into her lap. "I have something of importance to inform you of. Something I cannot allow Charles to overhear."

"Speak plainly, madam. What is the issue," I demanded. Why was she being so secretive? Should I be afraid?

She grimaced. "Miss Jane Bennet has travelled to London and is staying with her aunt and uncle. In Cheapside," she added snidely.

Had she come for Bingley? Did that… no. That did not mean she returned his affections. It could be her family sending her to chase after his five thousand a year!

"Has she called upon you?" I asked.

"Oh yes," she answered. "She was most eager to renew our acquaintance. And has invited me to visit her at her uncle's home," she grimaced at the thought.

I paced. What was going to happen? If we were to send Bingley to Europe, would she be sent to follow after him? Never allowed to escape her and her mother's clutches?

"Do not fret, Mr Darcy," Miss Bingley assured me. "I will ensure Miss Bennet is taken care of."

Taken care of? I stared at her from across the sitting room of the Bingley residence. What exactly did she mean by that? It sounded so… sinister. But then again, she is a lady. She probably meant it different… No, that might even make it worse. Ladies were vicious when they wanted to be.

But I could do nothing on this front. This was for Miss Bingley to handle at her discretion. It was not my place to interfere with how ladies did things.

I inclined my head to her in acknowledgement.

She smiled sweetly. With a hint of sour behind it.

"Darcy!" Charles burst through the doorway, a forced grin upon his mouth as he did. Sadness still lingering. "You are early, good man. What is the matter with you? I have never seen you arrive early for anything in my life."

I scoffed. "Are you now informing me that I am not welcomed into your home if I am to arrive earlier than agreed upon?"

"Nonsense! You can come an hour, or even six hours, earlier! I am sure we all would love that, right Caroline?"

"Hmm," she hummed. Her eyes twinkled at the prospect. "I do enjoy our little talks, Mr Darcy. We should aim to have more of them."

Dear God no!

My face betrayed my thoughts on this. Bingley laughed, uproarious, and came over to slap me on the back. Miss Bingley looked hurt, but smoothed it over quick. "What are your plans for the day?"

"I do believe that Darcy has come to collect me for some assistance in a matter of his," Bingley half explained.

I grimaced. "I asked if you wanted to accompany me and you agreed. You are not required to do any work for it."

"Oh? What is this matter?" Miss Bingley interrupted.

Bingley smiled. "His sister, Miss Darcy, is coming to London for a brief visit. And he is being the very good and kind brother and is organising for her to have a new piano forte for her to practise upon."

"You are a good brother indeed, Mr Darcy," Miss Bingley exclaimed. "So generous."

I waved my hand to dismiss this. Was it so good of me to do such a thing for my sister? Was it not something to be expected, that I provide for her and ensure she is happy? "We should go," I said.

Bingley chuckled at my discomfort. "Right, right. We will be back later, Caroline."

"Actually, Mr Darcy," she halted my escape. "I have had a wonderful idea. When your sister arrives, you should bring her for afternoon tea. I do wish to see Georgiana."

Bingley nodded. "That is a capital idea! Right, Darcy?"

I nodded. "I am sure she would like that very much. Thank you."

"Oh, do not be so formal, sir," she complained. "Our families are after all rather close." She flicked her eyes to Bingley, as if she was saying more to him.

Bingley cleared his throat. "Yes. Well, we should leave. Tradesmen do not like tardiness."

We did escape. But I wondered, what else did she mean? Was it something to do with…

"Ignore Caroline," Bingley interrupted as we left the house. "She has ideas and they are rather ridiculous."

"You're making me worry more," I calmly responded.

He huffed a sigh. "She has made suggestions that I need to distract myself to be able to move on from Miss." He trailed off on her name, as if speaking it would be a jinx. "Anyway. She thinks a distraction of a wedding would be helpful. Has mentioned it more and more now that we are in London."

"Whose wedding?"

He grimaced. "Do not force me to have to admit this out loud. Good man! I have no expectations of you or anything of the sort."

"Bingley," I snapped.

"Caroline wants you to make her an offer of marriage," he grimaced.

I stumbled over my feet.

Bingley caught my arm to keep me upright. "I know you are not interested in her and have been very much the opposite of attentive towards her. And I do not fault you that. One cannot force the heart to love when it does not wish to." He babbled on and on.

"Stop," I begged. "I am sorry you had to be put into the middle of this."

"My sisters liked you when they first met you. And Netherfield made them think you would make an excellent addition to the family."

I shuddered.

"You are my friend," he reiterated. "You do not have to marry my sister because she has her eyes set upon you."

I swallowed and thanked him. Why was he so good? I did not deserve such a friend. Here he was protecting me from his sister's scheming and I had… I had separated him from his heart's desire.

But she had not been… Damnation!

It would only serve to hurt him more if he was made aware of her being in town. He may even misinterpret this as her having interest in him

So, I did the kindest thing I could. I concealed the knowledge of her being there. Everything was going back to what it was meant to be. Everything was going to be fine.

I stopped myself from thinking of George and Elizabeth. Went about town with my friend. Did business when necessary.

Georgiana was an excellent distraction. She was all too happy to spend time with Bingley and his sisters. And they were happy to have her.

"Must I leave, brother?" she asked the night before she was to return to Pemberly.

I nodded. "You must."

"But," she pouted. "Will you not come home, too?"

Ah, my heart. Why did this child know how to squeeze it so and get me to react? "I will."

She perked up at this prospect.

"But, not yet," I informed her. Watched as her shoulders sagged in disappointment. "Soon," I promised.

"What is keeping you from Pemberly?" she asked.

At this I grimaced and told her of the letter demanding my presence at Rosings. It had arrived that morning. And I had been… well.

That morning I had groaned. "Ugh," I pinched the bridge of my nose and rubbed. "Please no!"

"Sir?" the butler stood by.

"I am needed at Rosings. My aunt has said so," I flourished the letter to him.

"Very well, sir. When do you leave?"

"Too soon," I groaned.

At this, the man actually chuckled. Had he not worked for my family for all my life, I would have taken some offence. Yet, he was well aware of all the going on in my family, had listened to my father moan about aunt on occasions.

And was well aware that he was not to allow that lady to step a foot inside of the London house for fear of never getting rid of her.

"Perhaps she has good tidings," he suggested.

I snorted. It was unlikely she would announce her death that easily.

At least I was not to suffer alone. "How did she manage to get you?" I asked my cousin in a hushed tone. "Don't you have a battalion to command?"

Colonel Fitzwilliam chortled at that. "You know Aunt. She may have threatened to find me on a battlefield if I did not come to her."

"Of course, she did."

"What is this?" Lady Catherine's voice boomed. "What are you two talking about? I demand to know!"

"The weather, Aunt," Colonel supplied smoothly. "We were commenting about how nice the weather has been."

I turned my eyes to the heavens and wished to be anywhere but here. Too many boot lickers hung around my aunt, all too happy to compliment and agree. No one dared challenge the great Lady Catherine de Bourgh. And she enjoyed meddling in other people's affairs too much.

If I had to hear one more time of how she wanted to help her nephew… I might flee the country.

"Fitzwilliam," she drew my attention. "You are awful quiet."

"Am I, Aunt?"

She narrowed her eyes at me, as if she could see through me to the truth. "How is your sister?"

"Georgiana is well."

"And she is of course practicing her piano."

"Everyday."

Aunt hummed and reminisced about her own lost chances of piano.

Anne nodded along with her mother. She did not speak. But she did look to me in a way that was… unsettling. What did she expect from me? I was not going to be able to save her. I did not dislike my cousin, I did not know her.

As soon as it was polite, Colonel Fitzwilliam and I excused ourselves for a walk about the grounds. One thing about Rosings, it had some very lovely walks. And we had explored many of them over the years. Knew them well.

"You need to watch out, cousin," the colonel warned.

"Why is that?"

"Because Aunt is about to throw Anne at you."

No madam, you shall not be saddling me with a bride. I can guarantee that union and any other you offer up will never occur. I shuddered. "Surely she realises that I am not marrying her daughter because she says that my parents had arranged it?" It was not written down in the will, thus I am under no obligation to fulfill it.

He laughed.

"Damn it." Great. I knew there was more to this invite than appeasing a lonely woman. She was scheming and I refused to be caught in her trap.

"Miss de Bourgh is of marrying age," cousin teased.

I shoulder checked him. "I do not have time for a wife."

"Says the man who has spent months out in the country gallivanting with friends. You should have pursued a career. Then you could use that excuse."

"I have been working," I fought back. Albeit it was not as time consuming or life altering as a career in the army. But there were endless correspondences, dealing with tenants, balancing books. Add in Georgiana to ensure her safety… it was not like I did nothing while at Netherfield.

"Have you considered finding your own bride," he suggested.

"Have you?" I snarked.

"Yes," he shot back easy. "I have been looking and thinking of how I could provide for a wife."

I blinked at him in shock. "And?"

"And I am not currently engaged."

"Ah," we continued to walk. In silence this time.

"Have you heard from George?"

I stumbled over my feet and stared at him. What had he said? Did he bring him up for some reason?

My cousin patted my shoulder. "He was like family to you. I can only guess as to how much it hurt for him to betray you."

It stung.

"I ran into him in the country… he'd joined the militia," I admitted.

"You spoke to him?"

"No."

"You don't forgive him?"

"He tried to run off with my sister," I snapped back. The old wound reopened and started to bleed out all the hurt and anger once more. "I trusted him." Then I frowned at my cousin. "Did you expect me to forgive and invite him back to Pemberly?"

"Yes."

"Well, you're wrong."

"It would seem so. As I said, he was like family. No-one would be surprised if you gave him another chance."

*

"Allow me to present, Miss Elizabeth Bennet," some-one introduced.

My heart stopped and may or may not have fallen out of my arse to the floor.

Miss Elizabeth… at Rosings… NOW?!

I turned and shuffled forward a little. Bringing her attention, her large expressive eyes, over to me where she looked as surprised to see me as I her.

"Mr Darcy?"

All the good breeding in me reminded me I had to do something; I bowed.

"You know my nephew?" Aunt queried.

Ah damn it. Of course, she would be dying to hear all the gossip. And unfortunately, Miss Elizabeth had ample ammunition. She could say a lot about me, some of it true in one sense, and a lot of it lies that other people believed completely.

"Yes, your ladyship," she spoke, careful of what she said. "We became acquainted during his stay at Netherfield."

"Is that so," she tried to fix her eyes on me, but I kept my chin held high and refuse to meet them.

Dinner was… an unusual event. Every word out of Miss Elizabeth exasperated my aunt. I shared a look with my cousin. No one, not even family, had ever dared to speak so candidly with this woman.

To be fair, Aunt dug rudely into Miss Elizabeth's background.

"All?! All your sisters are out before the eldest are married? That is highly unusual," Aunt showed her disdain for such a lack of protocol. "Your youngest sister must be very young."

"She is not yet sixteen." A cheeky smile curved the full lips of Miss Elizabeth. "But it would be very hard on younger sisters if they could not have their share of amusement because the eldest had yet to be married. It hardly encourages sisterly affection," she finished off.

I smothered a laugh into my napkin.

"Upon my word," Aunt exclaimed. "You give your opinion freely for someone so young… what is your age?"

"With three grown up younger sisters, you can hardly expect me to own up to it," she evaded.

"I insist I should know."

A hint of disdain pinched at Miss Elizabeth's features. I could not help but watch it. She spoke another language with her eyes and lips. Something that accentuated her words, added more to them.

"I am not one and twenty, ma'am," she answered politely.

For the rest of the meal, my aunt spoke to the others at the table.

Miss Elizabeth sank into her own thoughts, only occasionally responding when called upon. I wanted to ask her questions, see if she would engage with me and watch as her face started to speak on its own.

"Won't you play for us, Miss Bennet?" Aunt requested as we settled into the sitting room for the evening.

"Oh, please don't make me," Miss Elizabeth begged.

"I insist."

My cousin encouraged Miss Elizabeth towards the piano forte and offered to turn the sheet music. She played. It was hesitant and filled with errors. But I liked it. I liked hearing her play.

"You will never improve, Miss Bennet, unless you practice," Aunt chided her. "You may visit Rosings as much as you like and practice on the piano forte in Mrs Jenkinson's room." She nodded towards the governess. "You will be in nobody's way in that part of the house."

"Thank you, ma'am," Miss Elizabeth said with a slight laugh.

"There are few people in England who have true enjoyment in music like myself," Aunt began yet again to boast. Miss Elizabeth started to play another piece. Perhaps she was being smart and covering the sound of my aunt's voice.

I wandered away from the group and over to the piano forte.

Her eyes flicked from the sheet music to me, to the keys, then back to me. "Do you mean to frighten me, Mr Darcy, by coming in all this state to hear me?" Then she jerked her chin higher and smiled bright. "But I will not be alarmed. My courage always rises with every attempt to intimidate me."

"I know you find great enjoyment of professing opinions that are not your own," I told her. Intimidate? Me? Never.

She gasped. "Your cousin would teach you not to believe a word I say, Colonel Fitzwilliam." She spoke to him, eyes gleaming back at me. "That is ungenerous of him, is it not?"

"It is indeed," my cousin agreed.

"It provokes me to say things about his behaviour in Hertfordshire which may shock."

"I am not afraid of you," I countered.

"Perhaps you should be," she warned in good humour.

"What have you to accuse him of?" my cousin pushed. "I should like to know how he behaves amongst strangers."

"First time I ever saw Mr Darcy was at a ball where he only danced four dances. Though gentlemen were scarce and many young ladies were without partners."

She counted how many times I danced? Was the night that boring?

My cousin laughed.

"I'm sorry to pain you," she added. "But so it was."

"I can well imagine," he added.

"I am ill-qualified to recommend myself to strangers," I defended my actions.

Her teasing smile slipped and genuine… concern? Interest? "Shall we ask him why," she conspired with my cousin. "Why a man of sense and education, who has lived in the world, should find he is ill-qualified to recommend himself to strangers?"

Shared flesh and blood most certainly did not protect me from his prodding. "Come on, cousin."

I swallowed. "I…" I struggled to articulate it. "I don't have that talent," George came to mind. "To which some possess in conversing easily with strangers."

Miss Elizabeth softened. She smiled. "I do not play this instrument as well as I should wish to, but I have always supposed that to be my own fault. Because I would not take the trouble of practicing."

I nodded, a grimacing smile curving my own lips. "You are right. You have employed your time much better. Nobody hearing you play could hear anything wanting. We neither of us perform for strangers."

She lost her smile and looked to be taking the words to heart.

And there we stayed, staring at each other. Considering the meanings of our words a little more serious than we had intended.

"What are you talking about over there," Aunt demanded.

I looked heavenward. Why couldn't she leave well enough alone?

"What are you telling Miss Bennet? I must have my share in the conversation!"

And thus we were forced to return to entertaining the lady of the house.

*

"She would make a good wife," Cousin commented over our joint walk.

"Who?" I yawned.

"Miss Bennet."

"Are you planning on asking for her hand in marriage?" I was calm. Yes, I found her charming and handsome and I enjoyed her company. However, I was not silly enough to think I could ever capture her heart. She simply enjoyed teasing.

Rather similar to someone else I knew…

Cousin laughed. "Why would I do that to you?"

"What?" I stopped walking.

A few steps ahead, so did he, looking back at me like I had gone mad. "Did you think no one would notice?"

"Notice what?"

"That you are smitten for Miss Bennet."

I scoffed.

"You are! And it is clear as day."

Now that was a worry. And something new. I had never been 'clear as day' before in my life. That is exactly how George and I had never been caught. And why so many boys at school had mistaken my shyness for being cold.

"What exactly are you saying I am doing?" I demanded the particulars of my actions that had given me away.

"Staring adoringly," he started to list off. "Only participating willingly in conversations when she was part of them. Opening up emotionally," he added. "I would not be surprised if you picked a bouquet of flowers and gave them to her with a sonnet."

"Dear God," please, do not let me become so… sappy. "I need to leave."

"Why?" he changed paths.

I followed him without thinking. "Because I need to stop this ridiculousness."

"Why?"

I narrowed my eyes at him. "Do not tease, cousin," the warning made.

He chuckled and held his hands up in defence. "I only mean, why do you need to stop? Miss Bennet is not protesting. In fact, she seemed to rather enjoy your attentions."

"What?!"

"Truthfully," he stopped in the middle of the path and shook his head at me. "You are dense. Do you not see how the lady responds to your attention? How she fights back with her words and keeps the conversation going with you for as long as possible? Or how she looks at you?"

Did she?

What I had seen was someone who liked to always have the last word. To tease in a way that many did not realise due to their own ignorance. What I had seen were mischievous smiles. What I had seen…

Colonel Fitzwilliam clapped me on my back, hard, jolting me back into the present. "Would you look at that?"

I twisted my head to see… The home of the Colins'… and where Miss Elizabeth Bennet was staying.

Panic. I tried to run, but my cousin tightened his hand on my shoulder instead, holding me in place. "It would be rude of us not to drop in and say hello."

"Must we?" I all but begged.

He hummed and thought for a moment. "You're right."

I sighed. Of course, he would not push. He was my cousin, I could trust and rely on him.

"You can go inside and pay your respects and I'll head back to Rosings." He thumped my shoulder hard.

"You are not leaving me!" my brain scrambled. What was I going to do?! Ask to see her?! Have stilted conversation over tea with Mrs Colins there?! Horror!

"Oh, so you want to go back to Aunt and spend some quality time with her?" He sneered.

I narrowed my eyes at him in a glare. "You are cruel, cousin."

"And you are being a coward, Fitzwilliam. Do this. Try. Or someone else will come in and marry the girl you want and Aunt will wear you down and make you marry Anne!"

I grimaced. "Fine."

With that said, I went to the door and knocked. The servant informed me that only Miss Bennet was at home.

I did not know if I was lucky or unlucky.

I was shown into the small sitting room, where I bowed, and she curtseyed. "How are you this morning?" I asked.

"Very well, thank you," she smiled. "Would you like some tea?"

"No," I said automatically. "I cannot stay long." Or I may expire from sheer awkwardness.

She sank back down to her seat.

"And your parents, are they in good health?" Damn it, why did I sound so stupid?

"They are, thank you for asking."

"And your sisters?" If I could cut out my tongue, I would. Perhaps the letter opener before her would work. That would be a nice thing, if I did not have to ask for permission to use it.

"They are," she wet her lips with the tip of her tongue. "My eldest sister, Jane, has been in London for several months."

Oh shit.

"Did you happen to see her when you were there?" She asked.

Honestly, I answered. "No, I did not." And it was true, I had not laid eyes upon the lady. I did however know of her being in town, and that was information I did not offer up.

We were silent.

Awkward.

I did not know what to say or ask.

She was right, I had not practised. Bingley supplied conversation and George had been the charming one.

I did not and was not.

Escape! Now!

"Excuse me, I'll leave you," I bowed.

She flapped her hands in the air and opened her mouth as if she wanted me to stay, but I could not do this. I left.

Stalking back up the path, my heart raced. Why was that so hard to do?!

Ugh, she must think I am an idiot! Of course, she would not consider marrying such a man. She would prefer someone like George, someone who could put her at ease and entertain her with stories. Someone like Bingley who could be friendly with her mother and sisters and loved by everyone.

Marry? Why was I thinking like everyone else? And with her?

I did not dare go back into the house once I reached there. My cousin would pounce on me immediately and ask what had gone wrong for me to arrive so soon. I would not face my aunt either, so I continued walking alone with my thoughts.

Not ideal.

I cut across to the woods as far away from the Colins home and stalked.

Perhaps, I needed to be forthcoming with my intentions and allow her to find her answer. Give her no reason to doubt me and stop confusing everyone and ask for her hand in marriage. Then she can put me out of my misery and I can know if there is a reason to hope or to give up.

I crested the hill and breathed in deep.

Could I see myself married?

Maybe.

Did I have to marry?

Yes. I needed to provide a legitimate heir to Pemberly. And I wanted to have children… that was something I never admitted to George, it would have been cruel.

Could I marry to a woman? Bed one?

Hmm…

Could I if it was Elizabeth as my wife?

… Yes.

Could I love again? Love her and be a husband?

Well… that all depended upon her response. With the way her family were throwing Jane at Bingley, Elizabeth's answer may be 'yes' to give her family financial security. She may not be consenting because of her feelings. And that… hmm. I knew I could suffer through heartbreak, though I wanted to avoid it once more. But could I love her if that was the case?

Did I love Elizabeth? And is it the sort of love that I could marry with?

It took time for me to find the courage and the words. When I knew the Colins family was out, I visited Miss Elizabeth and hoped not to make too much of a fool of myself. An impossible task, but I wished to have some dignity in what I was about to embark upon.

Once again, I was shown to the sitting room, bowed and greeted her, refused tea.

Good Lord, I could not keep still. I paced and tried to remember what I had wanted to say. How do you persuade someone to consider tying their life to you for the rest of time? In a nervous outburst, I started. "In vain I have struggled," I swallowed and added, "it will not do. My feelings will not be repressed. You must allow me to tell you how ardently I admire and love," oh… I had never spoken those words to anyone else but George. "Love you." And they were true here too. "I love you." My chest felt warm and it was easy to say the words and mean them.

How did I doubt that I was growing to love this woman?

All the more reason for me to worry now.

Please do not let me fail in explaining this to her. Please, allow her to understand how overwhelming this is and how sincere I mean it.

"And declaring myself thus, I am fully aware I will be going against the wishes of my family, my friends, and I need not add, my better judgement." I do not care anymore, I want to let go and love. Please accept me as me. "The relative situation between our two families is as such, that any alliance must be regarded as a highly reprehensible connection. As a rational man I cannot ignore it. But it cannot be helped."

Elizabeth remained silent, watching with wide eyes of bewilderment.

No, I need to reassure her that I am dedicated to her.

I chose to… exaggerate a little. "Almost from the earliest moments of our acquaintance I have come to feel for you a passionate admiration and regard which despite all my struggles has overcome every rational objection." Not that early on, more of a steady growing affection that threatened to grow more with every passing day.

Dear God, can this be over soon? I want my heart to stop trying to bash its way out of my chest. For my knees to stop feeling like they are about to give out from under me, and for my breakfast to stay in my stomach.

"I beg you most fervently to relieve my suffering and consent to be my wife," the words left my mouth and that was it. That was all I could do to convince this woman to please consider matrimony with me.

I waited with my nerves in the silence after.

And waited more.

This silence was stretching beyond what was civil. Was she formulating a rejection? If she was going to say yes, wouldn't she have said it immediately? Wouldn't she have been joyous in my proposal and have put me out of this agony as soon as she could? Even a nod of her head would be a kindness.

Did she have no interest in me at all?

Was Bingley and my cousin wrong?

Elizabeth schooled her features and looked at me as if I were an acquaintance. Disinterested and polite. "In such cases as these, I believe the established mode is to express a sense of obligation." She took a moment before sniffing and continuing. "But I cannot. I have never desired your good opinion and you have bestowed it most unwillingly. I am sorry to cause pain to anyone but it was most unconsciously done and I hope it will not last long."

I was a fool.

A darn fool!

"This is all the reply I am to expect?" Why did this hurt so much? "I might wonder why with so little effort of civility I am rejected," I lashed out. Instead of taking her rejection on the chin and bidding her farewell, the way a gentleman would, I made demands of her and questioned her manners.

I should be ashamed of myself, had not the burning shame of rejection been the overriding emotion.

"And I might wonder why," she snapped back through clenched teeth. "With an evident desire to offend and insult me you chose to tell me you love me against your will. Was this not some excuse for some incivility?"

Well…

I guess my honesty of words was my downfall.

She continued, a fire appearing to have been lit within her to try to burn me in every way possible. "I have every reason in the world to think ill of you. Do you think any consideration would tempt me to accept the man who has been the means for ruining the happiness of a most beloved sister?"

Bingley. She knew about Bingley and Jane, how I kept them away from each other… how? Who could have told her?

"Can you deny you have done it?" she demanded. "That you have separated a young couple and caused unnecessary heartache?"

Unnecessary heartache? Ha! Towards Bingley I have been kinder than I have towards myself. "I have no wish to deny it. I did everything in my power to separate my friend from your sister. And I rejoice in my success."

"Why?" she gasped.

"Because I believed that Bingley was more attached to your sister than she to him. She showed him very little encouragement. I even suspect she was only acting out your mother's wishes and not her own."

"What?!" she exploded out of her seat and stalked over to me.

"I watched them carefully before acting. She was indifferent."

"My sister is shy and modest!" she defended.

Did she mean that… had Jane confided in her sister and been in love with Bingley all this time? That she had been acting of her own wishes and hopes and not on her scheming mother's designs?

"But it is not merely that for which my view of you was founded," Miss Elizabeth continued. "Long before, my opinion of you was set when Mr Wickham told me of your dealings with him and how you treated him so ill. How can you defend yourself on that?"

George you son of a bitch. What exactly have you been running around telling people?!

"You take an eager interest in that gentleman's concerns." Jealousy filled me. George was mine, not hers to ache after and desire. And… I wanted her attention to be on me, not him.

"Who cannot help but feel for him when they know of his misfortunes?" she continued.

"His misfortunes?" I scoffed. "Yes, his misfortunes have been great indeed." All self-inflicted and without consulting me on any of the consequences! Idiot! Damn it, George! You damn fool!

"And of your infliction," she accused me. "You have reduced him to his present state of poverty and yet you can treat his misfortunes with contempt and ridicule."

The devil George?! I made you poor?! I offered you everything! You had so many options, even if you did not want to stay by my side. You could have joined the church, could have studied law, could have done so much! But no, you chose to leave and now you blame me for your choices! This is all your own fault, George!

"And this is your opinion of me," I said in disbelief. Why did I waste my time on this woman? "My faults by this calculation, are heavy indeed."

She looked smug. I hated that.

"Perhaps these offenses may have been overlooked," I suggested nastily. "Had not your pride been hurt by the honest confessions of the principles that have long prevented me from forming any serious affection for you. Had I concealed my struggles and flattered you with sweet words. But disguise of any sort is my abhorrence." And the curse I must suffer.

She lost that smug look and looked ready to defend herself once more.

I did not give her the chance. Instead, I admitted without shame or guilt or nerves. What was the point now? She had rejected me and so it was of no consequence to admit everything had been my true emotions and thoughts. "Nor am I ashamed of the feelings I related, they were natural and just. Could you expect me to rejoice in the inferiority of your connections? To congratulate myself on the hope of relations whose conditions in life are so decidedly below my own?"

Oh, that was a cruel blow to deal.

"You are mistaken Mr Darcy." She glared. "The mode of your declaration merely spared me any concern I might have felt for refusing you had you behaved in a more gentleman like manner. Your arrogance and pride made me realise you are the last man I could ever be prevailed upon to marry!"

And there it was.

The end of our little story.

I had my answer and that was that. No more agonising… just returning to the old familiar heart ache.

"Forgive me, madam, for taking up so much of your time," I gave her a curt bow and exited as fast as I could.

The look on her face as I did… I can never forget it. The anger and disgust. Twisting her features. Distorting them.

The walk back to Rosings was hell. It did not clear my mind at all. She has rejected me and I should cut all ties and leave her alone. Yet… I needed to defend myself. I needed to set the record straight.

I do not think I can live in this world knowing that she thought ill of me.

Or rather, that she thought ill of me without me being able to explain myself first.

But if I was to go back and try, we would devolve into another round of arguing. More words than is necessary could come out in a fit of emotion.

What did George tell Miss Bennet? What was the story he had made up and shared? Yet again, he was doing as he pleased without consulting me on the topic or accepting my input. Please George, I trusted you.

Please, do not slander my family.

I wanted nothing more than to talk to him right now. See his face and know that it would be fine, hear his voice and laugh, feel his warmth as he held me. I ached for comfort.

I also wanted to shake him violently and force him to explain himself.

But that would never happen again. I had to suffer through this alone and make my next decision myself.

And that decision was simple to make; leave Rosings.

If I stayed, it would be clear in our next interactions that some event had occurred between us and ended badly. I could not predict how Miss Bennet would handle this. I did not wish to be nearby for when she informed her friends and family of my unprovoked proposal. How she refused me because there was defect in my being.

And to suffer the wrath of my aunt… no thank you. I did not want the lecture about marriage and how she expected me to choose better than Miss Bennet. How I was meant to be with my younger cousin, her daughter, instead.

But… I could not let go of Miss Elizabeth's condemnation. I could not forget of all that she had accused me of and barely allowed me to defend myself.

What was done was done, and it was done out of obligation to Bingley. I would do it again to spare him unnecessary suffering.

George however. I wished to know what he had said, how he had spun the tale and made himself into a victim.

The only victim in our story was Georgiana. The child that had believed her crush had loved her back and wanted to marry her. And that is because we have never been able to be completely honest with anyone about our situation.

George was never a victim, but he and I were to blame for it getting too far out of control. I more so.

I was to blame for it happening at all.

I should have watched over my sister better.

I should have been more supportive of George.

I should have done as he had wished all those years ago in school when he wanted to cut ties.

No matter what, I had to go and pack. I could not stay any longer near that woman.

I stalked inside of the house and headed for the stairs immediately. Even with the size of the house, my aunt heard and demanded to know who was there and what they were doing.

My cousin came out to placate her and looked at me in surprise. "Fitzwilliam?"

I shook my head at him. "I'm sorry, I need to go to my room."

"Is everything alright?"

"Who is it? Is it my nephew?" she yelled.

I apologised once more. "I cannot right now."

With a knowing look, he nodded at me. "Okay." Turning back around he went to mollify our aunt.

Gratitude swelled, then died very quick as I went to deal with my decision.

I began to pack. The valet that attended me entered the room and understood immediately. He took over in ensuring all my personal effects were stowed away into their travel cases.

I did not dare tell my aunt that evening. She would no doubt spend it hounding me about my decision and guilt me for wanting to leave her at all.

But what to do about the words roiling inside of me that I could not speak?

Glancing at the writing desk. Well, though I never wanted a permanent record of things, it would clear my name of some of the charges laid at my door. And it would quieten my mind.

I sank into the chair and looked at the blank parchment. How do I begin?

Is this the same waste of time as my proposal? Would it make very little difference to her?

No… this was not for her. This was for me. If I could articulate myself without getting emotional and off topic, admit and explain what I could. It would clear my conscience of what was weighing it down.

After that, I could do nothing more than hand it to her. If she burned it without reading, read it but disregarded it all. Shared it with other people… I would have to make a special request for it not to be made public knowledge.

Even as a half-truth, there would be information that I would not like to be shared with others.

I picked up the quill, carved at the tip to freshen it and opened the bottle of ink.

It took considerable time for me to pen my account. Emotionally, I was drained. With my sealed letter in hand, I escaped the house and started to walk, and was fortunate to see her on route.

"Miss Bennet," I addressed her. "Would you do me the honour of reading this letter?"

She did not speak, but took the letter.

I politely nodded and left. No more explanations. This was it. The final time I would ever see her and I had to accept that.

Back at the main house, I bid my aunt farewell.

Colonel Fitzwilliam looked at me confused. He tried to stop me and demand answers. I promised to write him, later.

"You better," he gave me slap on the back.

I gave him a tight smile and climbed into the carriage. Quick, before my aunt could make it outside, I escaped.

Enclosed inside the letter I gave to Miss Bennet, I recounted everything. Naturally, things were edited out. But at least I had been clear and honest in what I could admit to.

"To Miss Elizabeth Bennet,

"Be not alarmed upon receiving this letter, Madam. That it contains any renewal of those offers which were this evening so disgusting to you. I understand your feelings and will not push for you to alter them.

"That said, I must be allowed to defend myself against the charges laid against me. In particularly, concerning my involvement with Mr Wickham. For which if your accusations were true," *and madam, they most certainly are not!* "Would indeed be serious and grievous. But they are wholly without foundation and can only be refuted by me laying before you the connection Mr Wickham has had to my family and I.

"Mr Wickham is the son of a very respectable man who had the management of my family's estates. My own father was fond of him and held him in high esteem. Mr Wickham and I knew each other since childhood. We played together as boys and were as close as brothers. After his father's early death, my father supported Mr Wickham at school and afterwards at Cambridge. He had hopes he would make the church his career. But by then Mr Wickham's habits were as desolate as his manners were engaging.

"When my own father died, he ensured a comfortable family living for Mr Whickham should he choose to be ordained by the church. Mr Wickham declined any interest in such a profession and instead requested and was granted a lump sum of money as a replacement for the living.

"Mr Wickham chose not to maintain steady contact during this time, other than to come and ask for more money. All filial connection between us appeared to be dissolved and being now free of all restraint, his life was now of idleness and pleasure. How he lived, I knew not exactly, but one could assume as to the lifestyle he had chosen and the friends he spent his time with.

"But last summer our paths crossed once more under a most painful circumstance. This is what severed the last threads of our connection completely.

"My sister, Georgiana, who is twelve years my junior, was left to the protection of myself and Colonel Fitzwilliam after the death of our parents. She was in the care of Mrs Younge to further her education. But in whose character, we were most unhappily deceived.

"Under her supervision Mr Wickham had access to my sister. Georgiana was persuaded to believe herself in love and to consent to an elopement. She was only fifteen.

"A day or two before the intended elopement I joined them unexpectedly. Unable to conceal anything from her brother, she confessed to their plans at once and begged for my consent.

"I, of course, would never consent to such a union. Mr Wickham left the place immediately and cut all remaining ties he had with my family. It was not until Hertfordshire that we had seen each other once more. It was an unex-pected and unwelcomed renewing of acquaintance.

"This madam, is a faithful narrative of all my dealings with Mr Wickham. I can appeal to the testimony of Colonel Fitzwilliam who is aware of these transactions."

"I know not of what falsehoods that Mr Wickham im-posed himself upon you yet I hope you will acquit me of cruelty towards him hereafter. I gave ample opportunity and resources for Mr Wickham to live a good and respect-able life. Insinuating otherwise, is completely unfair.

"As to the other charge centred at me, is that regardless of the sentiments of either party, I detached Mr Bingley from your sister. I have no desire to deny this nor do I blame myself for any heartache that occurred. I had not been long in Hertfordshire before I became aware that Mr Bingley admired your sister. Though, it was not until the dance at Netherfield where I detected a serious attachment on his side. His partiality was clear in his true feelings and intentions towards her.

"Though she received his attentions with a kind smile and word, I did not detect anything more beyond that. I did not believe her to be indifferent because I wished it. I be-lieved it on impartial conviction.

"As to my objections to a possible marriage between the two, the situation of your family, though far from ideal was nothing in comparison with the total wont of propriety portrayed by your mother, three younger sisters, and on oc-casion, your father. You and your sister must be exempted from this. But it is clear that your mother had wanted your sister to pursue Bingley for his fortune, and not because of any feelings of love and affection. For that, I could not stand to see my friend suffer a loveless marriage of financial convenience. It is too cruel.

"My friend was easy enough to persuade to leave Netherfield soon after. I engaged in pointing out the certain evils of his choice of bride and it was not difficult to convince him of your sister's indifference of him.

"I cannot blame myself for doing this. There is but one part of my conduct in this affair I am not proud of. That is, I concealed from Mr Bingley your sister being in town. Perhaps this concealment was beneath me. It is done however, and was done with the best intentions at the time.

"And on this subject, I have nothing more to say and no other apology to offer."

"Yours sincerely,

Fitzwilliam Darcy."

This was the clean break from her and nothing more. I said my piece and was concise in doing so.

From here… there would never be anything else. We had nothing connecting us. No friends in common, we lived miles apart, our social circles were vastly different. There would never be a reason for us to cross paths once more.

And thus, I could do my best to forget her and the feelings I had once felt again.

I always believed that with time, past hurts were healed. That it provided the necessary distance for impartial assessment of the situation. And that vivid memories and feelings faded and were replaced with new experiences.

It did not. Which was absolutely fine. So fine. I always like to suffer in my angst. In fact, it showed how empty my life was.

I must return to my place in the world and not bother the people I had attached myself to any further. This is how it is meant to end.

What… the Devil?! What on Earth was this woman doing here? In my home?! Stepping foot on the grounds of Pemberly and walking about like she had no cares in the world?!

She looked… happy. Small smile playing on the edges of her lips, like she was struggling to keep it at bay and not show it to the world at large. Eyes gleaming as she looked around. And an ease that showed she was very comfortable indeed being there.

Then her head turned and gaze landed upon me. "Mr Darcy?"

What? Was she surprised to find me at my own home? I wanted to laugh, but the shock of seeing her there meant nothing else could compete with it. "Miss Bennet…" I had to remember my manners and bow to her.

She too, must have forgotten what was now second nature to us both, and bobbed a curtsey that lacked her usual smooth movement.

"Are your parents well?" I asked… because I could not think of anything else!

She opened her mouth, words not coming at first, before saying. "Yes. Very well. Thank you."

We stared at one another.

Clearly, this was unexpected. In no way had I thought I would see Miss Bennet ever again. And especially not here of all places.

An embarrassed silence fell over us.

Then we both went to speak. I did not know what to say to her and was happy to allow her to go first.

"I am sorry. The housekeeper informed us that all the family was away from home. We would never have intruded upon you if we had known."

"It's perfectly fine," I reassured. "I rode ahead of my guests to prepare. They come tomorrow. My sister and Mr Bingley and his sisters."

"Oh," she sighed.

"May I…" I started to say. "May I walk with you?"

She smiled, it was sweet and warm and very inviting. "Please," she nodded.

Through the gardens we wandered and though the words did not flow easy as I hoped, they came. We both asked questions of each other and answered. There was a strange sense of peace.

"Are you staying nearby?"

She nodded. "Yes, in Lambton. My aunt is from there. We are staying at the inn."

I nodded. "For how long are you in this part of the country?"

She looked up at me from under her lashes. "A while longer."

"Then…" I swallowed my words.

"Then?" she prompted.

Clearing my throat, I tried again, slightly different this time. "Would you like to meet my sister?"

"Oh, I think I would like that very much."

Smiles. Smiles on both of us. And shy and innocent little looks that we could not hold for long before we glanced away. But like magnets our eyes came back to each other.

It made me giddy and start to wonder if I could hope. Even though we had left on the worst possible terms at Rosings and she was very clear in her opinion on me.

But everything was different all of a sudden.

"How do you like Pemberly?"

"Like?" she widened her eyes in bewilderment at such a term. "It is magnificent. I love it."

"I'm glad you do." Pride filled my chest. I wanted her to like my home, to see it the way that I did as some place that is a privilege to call home.

"Why would you care about my opinion?"

"Because…" I love you? No. Hope might be there giving me a little push forward, but I could not be so presumptuous and put her on the spot. "I value your good opinion. It is not bestowed easily and thus it makes it all the more worth having."

Miss Elizabeth flushed violently. "I have to apologise."

"Please," I tried to cut her off before she could.

But she looked at me earnestly and I relented and allowed her to continue. "I had assumed that Mr Wickham had been telling the truth when he told me of your interactions together. And with the general opinion of you in Hertfordshire being less than agreeable, it was easy for me to believe him," she grimaced. "I am so sorry for that. And to have thrown it back at you was cruel of me."

"Do not worry," I wanted to comfort her with my hand on her arm, but that was too familiar. We were only acquaintances. So, I clasped my hands behind my back to restrain myself. "I can understand. And I am most certainly not innocent with some of the things I had said in retaliation."

She giggled.

Dear God!

The woman giggled. And I had made her do so. Even if she was to laugh at my expense, I wanted to hear it again.

We began to head back towards the house and to a couple I had never met before.

"Will you allow me to introduce you to my aunt and uncle?" she asked.

"I would be most honoured."

We came to the pair and I was so damn nervous. I did not want a repeat of Hertfordshire at all. And for that, I knew I had to try. I had to be more than polite and expect them to either accept me or to shun me. I needed to be friendly and engaging. The horror!

"Aunt and Uncle, this is Mr Darcy. Mr Darcy, this is my aunt and uncle, Mr and Mrs Gardiner."

"It is a pleasure," I bowed to the couple. "Mis Bennet has informed me you are staying in Lambton."

"Yes," Mrs Gardiner smiled. "I grew up there."

"It is a lovely village. I use to frequent it."

"I am so glad you think so," she said.

"Would it be alright, if my friends and I were to call upon you tomorrow afternoon? Do you think you will be at the Inn then?" I asked Miss Bennet.

Miss Bennet shared a look with Mr and Mrs Gardiner before answering. "We will be at the inn and be very happy to see you."

I swallowed and nodded. After bidding them goodbye, I strode into the house and nearly collapsed.

"Master, are you alright?" the housekeeper bustled over.

I attempted to wave her off, but she knew better. Hovered over me until I straightened and reassured her, I was in perfect health. "We had guests, it seems," I said.

She nodded. "The young miss in the party said she knew you and Mr Wickham."

"Miss Bennet. And I saw them on my way in."

She could no longer reach up to ruffle my hair in affection, so instead she patted my arm. I happily leant into it.

Then we went to business. Not that I needed to worry. The housekeeper was efficient and knew exactly what was required of her and the staff. Rooms were already prepared, meals organised, and everything as it should be.

"Thank you," I said to her.

*

The carriage arrived mid-morning containing my sister and Mr Bingley, Miss Bingley, and Mr and Mrs Hurst.

Georgiana glowed with happiness to be back at home. "Brother!" she leapt into my arms as soon as she entered the sitting room.

I laughed and squeezed her tight.

Bingley came in and we hugged one another with great slaps on each other's backs.

The others followed and were cordially polite. They began to recount the trip and everything I had missed by going off early.

To my sister and Bingley, I informed them of an engagement I had made on their behalf. "Miss Elizabeth Bennet is visiting the area with her aunt and uncle. I ran into them yesterday and asked if we may call upon them."

Bingley broke into a massive grin.

But we all were waiting on Georgiana.

She knew of Miss Bennet. Maybe she suspected something more was there, but she had been very good and never asked me about it. Simply ate up every description and recount of my time in Hertfordshire. She loved listening to Bingley tell the stories, because he tried to paint me in a better light than I would do.

But Georgiana had expressed an interest in meeting Miss Bennet. *"She sounds like an interesting lady,"* she had said.

Now, with the prospect of actually meeting, Georgiana nodded, eager.

*

"Your smile is back," Georgiana commented in private.

I frowned at her. "What?"

"You stopped smiling. For a long time," she explained. She sat at her piano to show me the new song she had learned. But instead, she started to talk about my smile?

"Miss Bennet must be special," she suggested.

I coughed and turned away so she would not see my face. "Miss Bennet is…" well, Hell. "Yes. She is."

Georgiana laughed. "I am glad, brother."

I did not have the heart to try and explain to her that Miss Bennet would not be joining our family. That this visit to Lambton was friendly and I was not getting my hopes up at all.

"She is a friend, Georgiana," I did manage to warn.

She grinned at me with a knowing look. "Whatever you say, Fitzwilliam."

Brat.

*

At the inn, the servant showed us to the sitting room Miss Bennet and the Gardiners were using. Introductions made. Everything went well. Bingley was eager in conversations with Miss Bennet and guilt niggled away at me as I watched them.

He was an excellent friend.

I needed to make amends for what I had done. No matter my intentions at the time, it had not been proper for me to have stepped between Bingley and his happiness.

If Georgiana had noticed my smile returning, I noticed Bingley was revived and breathing once more.

Georgiana tugged on my sleeve.

"Hmm?"

She motioned for me to give her my ear.

I lowered my head to hear her whisper her request. "Okay," I nodded my consent.

Fidgeting hands and slow steps forward, Georgiana went to Miss Bennet. "Miss Bennet, would you and your friends care to join us for dinner at Pemberly tonight?"

God bless the warmth that Miss Bennet radiated, putting my sister at ease. "We would be very honoured. Thank you."

Georgiana's shoulders released and she stopped fidgeting.

It was clear to all in the room that had taken a lot of courage and effort for such a child to ask. And the reward was worth it. She stayed close to Miss Bennet and joined the conversation easily. Of course, it was easy with Miss Bennet being so charming and engaging.

Mrs Gardiner joined them and I relaxed, glad that she was safe and happy amongst these new friends.

Bingley came over to me and sighed. "Doesn't this remind you a little of Netherfield?"

I cocked my brow at him. Of course, there were some sort of reminders, but I was glad it was not Netherfield. No, here in this tiny inn was far warmer and more welcoming.

But I did nod to him in acknowledgement. Especially since I could see that he wished the company of another Bennet girl.

We spent over an hour talking over tea before it was time for us to leave. Which was fine, of course, we would see them again soon for dinner. Georgiana barely contained her excitement in the carriage on the way back. She prattled on and on about the wonderful conversations she had. Bingley was just as eager and enthused to share their most recent memories.

I was starting to develop a headache from it all, but was pleased to see my sister happy.

"And Miss Bennet is so pretty!" she exclaimed.

Bingley shot me a grin. "Very pretty indeed. Right, Darcy?"

"Perhaps I should have walked myself home," I dead-panned.

The two laughed, knowing exactly what they were do-ing and how much I did not wish to discuss it right then.

Luckily, we arrived at Pemberly and Georgiana ran to inform the housekeeper of our expected guests for dinner. Like a good little mistress of the house.

I made a beeline for my office. A bland excuse of busi-ness given as an apology and closed the door on all the noise and people in my home. Then I sagged against the wood.

What on earth was I doing?! What was I thinking?!

Everyone around us was now very much aware of my feelings for Miss Elizabeth. And were going to be very sur-prised when nothing comes from it. When I do not renew my proposal to her.

I went to the side table and poured a generous glass, hissing as the alcohol hit the back of my throat.

Yes, a pleasant evening.

*

Dinner was a pleasant time. Miss Bennet and the Gardiners arrived and we had a nice chat before going into the dining room and eating. Nothing of unusual note occurred.

Afterwards, as we all went to continue our conversations in the sitting room, Miss Bingley said something rather alarming.

Even knowing that I had issues with the gentleman, she went and spoke his name under my roof. It was rude of her.

"You and your sisters must be bereft, Miss Elizabeth, now that the militia have left Hertfordshire." Miss Bingley had started as I walked in with my sister.

"Not at all," Miss Bennet replied.

"I know that you must be missing the company of one officer in particular. A Mr Wickham," she added.

I placed a hand on Georgiana's back and propelled her to the piano forte. Hoping to get her distracted so as to not have to listen to this talk.

Miss Bennet, however, was an angel. She smiled tight and excused herself. "Miss Darcy, let me help you by turning the sheets."

I came to a standstill in the middle of the room.

Bingley appeared before me and handed me a glass. "You alright, Darcy?"

"Quite so," I assured him.

I relaxed.

Miss Elizabeth Bennet was magnificent. She could counter someone else's comments, glide out of a situation with grace, did not need to be asked to help because she did what was right.

And as I watched the performance, I stared at her, the corners of my lips tugging up as I did.

Afterwards, we all applauded and the pair came to sit with us and join the conversation again. Though, it seemed they were having their own talk.

"Do you play?" Georgiana asked.

Miss Bennet laughed. "A little and not at all well. Your brother spent a whole evening having to suffer through my playing."

"Oh, but he says you play so well!"

I flushed as Miss Bennet looked to me. "I said you played well," I defended. Emphasis on 'well' being passable.

Her cheeky smile and glimmer of mirth in her eyes appeared. "Well? I will take that as a compliment and a fair assessment."

"As you should," a slight laugh entered my tone.

"Won't you play for us, Miss Bennet?" my sister pushed.

Now, she looked panicked.

"I would love to hear it," Georgiana added.

"I would rather not torture our present company," she tried very hard to avoid having to do as she was asked.

But she relented when Georgiana continued to push, Mr Bingley asked to hear, and finally, when I asked too.

Then she returned to the piano with my sister and played for us a short piece.

I enjoyed our evening immensely. And began to wonder if this is what it would have been like if that proposal had been accepted. Would we spend our evenings in this room talking and playing music? Would we be listening to our children playing piano for us before they go up to the nursery and bed? Would we laugh and argue and share inside jokes? Would we slip upstairs to the master bedroom and share kisses while we 'got ready for bed' but get lost in one another?

I would not ask her again to marry me without proper encouragement from her.

So it was pointless daydreaming.

The evening ended and we saw the Gardiners and Miss Bennet to the carriage. I kind of wished to have invited them to spend the rest of their stay at Pemberly. But that would be too forward.

Once we had returned to the others in the sitting room, the pleasant evening soured.

Miss Bingley once again spoke in her mean manner, this time about Miss Bennet. She complained about her looks and how shocking it was for a lady to be so brown, blamed it upon the travelling.

"I did not note that. I saw a healthy glow," I said.

Bingley agreed with me.

"I think I remember you saying that you thought her pretty, once, Mr Darcy," Miss Bingley continued. "I cannot say I agree with that statement now."

Mrs Hurst laughed with her.

At this, I narrowed my eyes at the ladies and sneered. "Yes, I did once think she was only pretty. But that was long ago. Now, after getting to know her character and spending many pleasant evenings in her company I would change that assessment. I believe she is one of, if not the most, handsome women I have the pleasure to be acquainted with!"

They shut up.

And rightly so. If it were not for the fact, they were the family of my dear friend, I would never allow them to set foot inside my home ever again. However, they were Bingley's sisters, so I gave them a curt nod and excused myself for the night.

*

Sleep had come very late for me indeed. And not easy at all. But I was eager to leap out of bed and dress, wearing the set of clothes that my valet laid out. Making some changes to wear my favourite colours.

It was like I was bubbling over with energy and excitement. I knew already that I wished to call upon Miss Bennet and ask if her and the Gardiners would like to join us once more. I was being greedy and wanting to squeeze as much time with her as I could from this.

I was the first to breakfast and enjoyed that solitude. Especially, when the housekeeper bustled in and chided me for scoffing down my meal as if I were ten once more.

Bingley came in. "Darcy? Good heavens, you are awake early!"

"Don't sound so shocked, man."

He chuckled and sat down. "You, friend, are hardly a morning person."

"Yes, well. I want to go and call upon Miss Bennet early, ask if she and the Gardiners would like to spend the afternoon here. Maybe even offer her uncle to fish."

Bingley smirked and nodded. "That sounds like a capital idea."

"Would you like to join me this morning?" I asked him.

He paused for a moment to consider. "Actually, no. I will stay here."

I frowned at him.

He shook his head. "I do not want to monopolise Miss Bennet's attention. And I think what you are doing right now is very good for you."

"What exactly are you saying?" I asked, suspicious.

"You are engaging in conversations with people you have only recently met. This is the first time I have met this charming sort of Darcy. At Netherfield, you use to sit back and let me do all the talking, not that I hated it," he laughed. "But you look as if you are trying to be… more."

"And is that bad?"

"Not at all, man! I am so glad to know you can make friends on your own without being the one chosen."

"Is that how you think we became friends?" I queried.

He nodded quick. "Absolutely! I spoke to you and did not leave you alone as soon as I found out you had no friends at school. I chose you to be my friend."

Groaning, I slumped back into the chair.

"You cannot deny it!" he teased.

I kicked him under the table, but that only served to make him laugh even more.

"I'm leaving," I told him and stood.

"Have fun!" he called after as I escaped.

Damn him and his good nature. I grinned as I left the house and went to the stables for my horse.

Chapter Thirteen; Mrs George Wickham

I was floating on the way to Lambton. The day was lovely, I was going to see Miss Elizabeth, nothing could go wrong.

"Miss Bennet?!" I exclaimed when I found her crying. "What is the matter?"

She sobbed, tried to recover herself, but failed and continued to cry uncontrollably. "My uncle… I need my uncle." She forced out.

I immediately took her elbow and directed her to a chair. "Where is he?" I asked her.

"He… they went walking towards the church…" she hiccupped.

Raising my voice, I called for the servant girl who had shown me in. She stared in horror but did as I requested of her, racing off to fetch Mr and Mrs Gardiner back.

That left us alone and… God, I had never felt so useless before in my life. I fussed and hovered, before dropping to my knee before her and asking if she needed a doctor or something to drink, anything. Please, Elizabeth, how can I help you?!

She refused. In her grasp, she held a scrunched-up letter. "I assure you, sir, I am well."

"I disagree with that statement," I countered, but held myself back. "What can I do to help?" It was amazing how steady my voice was even though my emotions were in turmoil in response. I needed to do something. Needed to fix this. Needed to protect her.

My hands fidgeted so as not to reach out and hold onto her own.

"I'm afraid there is nothing any of us can do." She bowed under the weight of her own pain and I could not help it any more, I surged up and hugged her. Held her small fragile frame as she shook with her tears.

It took a minute, but it felt like eternity, my heart being ripped from my chest as I waited over and over and over. Then she pulled back and sniffled.

I ripped my kerchief from my pocket and handed it to her.

"Madam," I attempted to be calm and get her to focus to explain what was the matter, what had caused her so much anguish. If not so I could fix it, so her uncle could be informed immediately and take care of it all post haste! "What is the matter?"

"I have received the most distressing news from Jane," she took a breath to collect her words. "She has written to tell me to come home immediately and for my uncle to assist my father in London in his search."

Search? What could have happened?

She inhaled and looking me in the eye, uttered a sentence I had never thought I would ever have to hear in my life. "My youngest sister, Lydia, has left her friends and everyone that she knows in Brighton and has run off… to elope with Mr Wickham."

George… George had run off with another young girl to marry her?! The damn fool!

I stood and began to pace. What was he thinking?! What on earth was he thinking he was going to achieve by doing this? Was he even thinking? I wanted to… oh I wanted to beat some sense into him.

"They've been tracked as far as London," Elizabeth continued to speak. "But no further. It seems they have no real intention of marrying and instead…" she broke off.

I looked to the heavens. Come on, now would be an excellent time to give some divine intervention.

"We fear she is lost forever."

My eyes closed and I had to take a steadying breath so as to not let my rage out there. She needed me to be calm. Losing it now, would not help anyone. I needed to be calm and to think things through.

"I should've done more to stop Father from allowing her to go to Brighton, I should've convinced him harder, proven Mr Wickham to be…"

"No," I snapped. "No, this is not your fault at all. Do not even think that for a moment, Miss Bennet."

"She has nothing. She has no friends, no connections, no money… and after this, she will be ruined." She gasped. "We're all ruined because of this."

Oh, no. I will not allow such a thing to happen. Not to her… not to anyone. George, you know better than this to include other people.

"I am sorry to have involved you in this," she admitted.

"Don't be… but I will make your apologises to my sister who wanted to invite you once more to Pemberly."

"Ah, yes," she gave a watery smile, then lost it. "We will be leaving immediately, as soon as my aunt and uncle return."

I nodded.

"If you could be so kind…"

I waited.

"As to conceal…"

"Of course." Even if she had not asked, I would have been willing to take this to the grave.

"I know it is impossible, but I would like to try and keep this news quiet and for those who need to know."

I nodded. "You have my word." And as I said that, I knew I was promising her something else. I would stay silent. But I would also do everything in my power to help discover George and Miss Lydia Bennet. I would fix this. Even if I had to drag George to a church and force him to marry… Dear God! What a ridiculous notion now.

"I will go," I bowed to her.

"Thank you, Mr Darcy."

And then I left her there to hurt on her own and wait for the Gardiners to arrive. I could do no more for her in that inn. But I could do more once I made it to London.

I hurried back to Pemberly and barked orders to the staff. Messages to be sent to people I trusted in town as I jotted them down.

Bingley came to me in amongst the chaos. "Good god man, what is the matter?"

"I have been called to London on business and leave this hour." I told him between the gulps of wine the house keeper forced on me with bites of food as I continued to write letters.

In none of them did I mention anything beyond the necessary information. Though these were trusted people for whom I knew could help me in my search, they were not people Miss Bennet knew and had not given me leave to share all the details. But I needed to begin somewhere with this search and asking for information about George was where I could begin.

"I am sorry, Bingley," I told him. "I will talk to you after all this has been settled… I have important information for you. But only after this is all settled and done."

He landed his hand heavy onto my shoulder and squeezed. "Okay. We will see you then."

I left Georgiana to deal with our guests. Did not even bother to give anyone else a proper farewell before I was on my horse and flying to town.

There, I began the search.

What surprised me the most was how easy it was to find them when I tried. George still inhabited the same establishments from when we were younger… it was laughable.

I forced my way inside of the building they had set up home and refused to leave.

It was in their bedroom that I found them lolling about in the middle of the day as if nothing mattered and they were enjoying life.

George.

He looked wrecked. Half dressed, bags under his eyes, a shadow of a beard growing in… and he reeked. Cheap perfume clung to him, along with body odour, and alcohol. He sat at the table littered with half eaten food, bottles of wine and used goblets.

"Fitz?" he blinked at me blearily.

Miss Lydia threw a dressing gown in haste over her chemise. Though she giggled as she did, she tried to look scandalised to be caught so undressed.

"George," I greeted him coldly. I ignored her completely for the moment.

"What are you doing here?" he stumbled to his feet and started to move as if he was going to embrace me.

I pushed him back. The first time I had touched him in so long and it was to keep him away? What more… this shadow of a man really was George. "I've come to clean up this mess you two are in."

"Mess?" Lydia Bennet gasped. "We are in love!"

Sure, like I would believe that. Even George looked heavenward at that statement.

"Do you have any idea about what you have done?" I directed my question at George.

But it was Miss Bennet, who slithered over, draped her hands all along his chest and gazed at him, that answered. "I've caught myself a husband." She simpered.

"Have you been to Gretna Green, then?" I asked her. Maybe a little cruel.

She pouted. "Not yet. But soon. Right, darling?"

George pushed her away as if her touch was revolting. "Right," he mumbled.

Did he not plan this? Did he have any intention of doing what was right? Or was he planning on having some strange fun, continue to build his awful reputation, and then leave a lady ruined in his wake? Destroying any footing she had in society along with that of her family?

George you stupid, selfish son of a bitch!

"What?" she snapped at me. "We are going to be married. We are just having some fun before we go do it. And it is all such a good joke to be playing on everyone back home. I can imagine their faces when I come back as Mrs George Wickham! Oh, I cannot wait!"

"This is not a joke, madam," I spoke cold to her. "Your family has been worried sick over your disappearance. There are consequences of your actions and many people will be hurt because of them." I looked at George as I said that last part.

He at least had the decency to look ashamed.

Lydia scoffed. "Lizzie will get over it. Anyway, George is mine now, right darling?" She cooed.

Oh, dear child… I wanted to snap at her. Those were most certainly not the right words to be speaking in my presence. If I were a petty man, I would tell her exactly what she had 'won' when she ran off with George. But I was a gentleman and George, no matter how idiotic he was acting, did not deserve to be outed so.

Not to mention, this girl was not someone to be trusted with anything, let alone a secret love affair between men.

Like he was waking up, George straightened his shoulders and cleared his throat. "Leave us, Lydia."

She did not even notice the change. But at least she did as requested. Only after she dropped a kiss to his lips.

I was sickened.

The door shut after her and we were silent. Neither of us ready to speak. And to think, this was the first time we had been alone since we had ended things. Over a year of not talking. But now, the words would not be about us, they were to be about him and his soon to be wife.

He went to the table and poured himself wine. Silently, offered me one.

I declined with a shake of my head.

Outside, the sounds of London floated in. Only muffled through the glass windows.

"You're an idiot," I told him.

George scoffed. "And?"

I shot him a glare. "And? That is all you can come up with?"

"What do you want from me, Darcy?"

"What do I want?"

"Yes! What do you want? You are the one who is here and making out like you are holier than thou! So, what the devil do you want?!"

"I can't have what I want and you know it!" I snarled back. "Damn it, George! You have no fucking clue!"

He gave a humourless laugh and drank from the cup. "Whatever, Darcy."

That bloody name! Why did he use that?! Why was he so determined to provoke me? "You are an adult, George. She is a child. Even though I want to yell at her for being so stupid, it is you who has been irresponsible. Taken advantage of someone so young."

At this he snorted his wine, then coughed as it went down the wrong way. "Well, colour me surprised. I thought the reason why you objected to my first choice of bride was the fact it was your sister. But it is the age. Tell me, if I had run off with Miss Elizabeth Bennet, would you still object?"

"Shut up."

"No."

"George," I warned him.

"Why? What are you going to do about it? Give me a good thrashing? Maybe that is what I want. Maybe I want to feel your hands on my body," he sneered. "Knock me down and really let me have it."

I stalked away from him.

"Playing rough no longer appealing, Darcy? Or are you trying to hide your hard cock from me?"

I looked back over at him in bewilderment. "What is wrong with you?"

"What isn't?" he swung his hands out, wine spilling from the goblet as he did. "I like men, not women. I am still pathetically in love with you. And nothing has gone right in my life in years. Tell me, is that all that is wrong or did I miss something?"

I pinched the bridge of my nose and gritted my teeth. "If that is the case, how the hell did you run off with a girl and give her the impression you we are going to take her to Scotland and marry her? Hm?"

"She is stupid!" George laughed as he yelled. "A silly stupid girl! Haha!"

"Do not say that," I hissed, getting closer to losing my temper completely.

"Why? It is the truth. She does not see it, does not want to. I could be bent over the breakfast table like a common whore and she would not see it as she stuffed her face with crumpets."

Now I lost it. The image George was painting… of a nameless man doing something like that to him… to my George?

Teeth bared, I knocked the goblet from George's hand and shoved him hard so his back ran into the wall behind him. "Enough!"

Blinking in confusion, George wobbled. "Fitz…"

Ah… Hell.

I forced myself back. Fussed over my clothes to make sure they were presentable, as if I had messed them up with two simple movements. Because if I stayed near, if I leaned in, if I melted into George… well… that was over and it would do no-one any good to revisit it.

And it would not be fair to Miss Elizabeth Bennet.

Even if she was no longer receptive to my affections.

No point in going back to an old… love. An old love. Old as in past. No more. Get that through your head, Fitzwilliam!

I sighed. "Lydia Bennet is going to be your wife."

George took a moment, struggling to keep up. Then he started to utter. "If you marry her sister, Elizabeth…"

"No," my answer was short.

"Why? We would have the perfect protection. We would be brothers-in-law and no-one could ever suspect. What am I doing wrong?!"

Scrubbing my hand over my face, I answered. "I cannot accept using other people like that. It hurts them. And it hurts me."

George's face showed so many emotions; hurt and confusion and anger and finally, disgust. "So, we will be… after all we have done. All of what we have been for each other and have felt? We will just be…"

I closed my eyes as he spoke, unable to watch any longer. "Brothers."

"That's horse shit."

"You don't think I've spent all my life wishing for things to be different?" I snapped.

"Things like me?" George hissed.

"Never." That was never what I meant. "Like the world. Our positions in life."

George sighed. Pushing away from the wall he bent at the waist and scooped up the now empty goblet. "I would have been happy to have been born in ancient times with you," he said as he straightened, a little wobble as he did.

I smirked. "You would have made a better Achilles." Of course, he understood the meaning behind the words, the implications of them.

"And you Patroclus."

For a moment, we smiled at one another.

"I would not change you," I admitted. "Never." Not even when he hurt me or when he chose to take on the world on his own and go through with his plans without consulting me first. I would not change George.

"What now?" he asked.

"Now," I sighed. "You get married."

"The fault lies with me, Mr Gardiner, so I should be the one to bear the cost," I had argued before the wedding day.

The Gardiners looked confused. "Even so, she is my niece," Mr Gardiner had protested. "She is my family and my responsibility."

I shook my head. "And Mr Wickham is my responsibility. I will not be swayed in this matter."

He shared one more look with his wife before giving in and shaking my hand on the matter. "Fine."

"Good." I was doing everything in my power to make sure it was all over and we could never go back to anything like before. So, I went about arranging the wedding. George was detained in my London home and not allowed near any alcohol.

Lydia was staying with her aunt and uncle.

The next time they would see each other would be at the altar. Even if I had to tie George to a pew to get him to go through with this. They would be married.

"Fitz," he had tried to talk to me in the carriage as we went to the church.

"What?"

"I…" he trailed off and shut his mouth. "I'm…"

Sorry? Was he going to apologise and think that was all that was needed for him to be forgiven? I scoffed.

He frowned at me.

"George," Leaning forward, I made sure her could hear every syllable I was about to make, so it was crystal clear to him. "You are a stupid bastard and I do not think I could ever stand to see your face ever again."

He opened his mouth to protest.

But I continued. "You have hurt me for years. And now this…" I hissed. "Nothing could make me forgive you for this."

He made no protest.

In the church, he went and waited. I stood by his side as his best man. I never thought I would be playing this role for George. Maybe in my most romantic of daydreams I had wished that we could have gone to a holy place and made whispered promises to one another.

God, I was an idiot.

Miss Lydia grinned and giggled as her uncle walked her down the aisle.

Twenty minutes later, they were announced Mr and Mrs George Wickham. I walked away from them for good.

*

A week later, I received a letter from my aunt. In it, she ordered me not to make Miss Elizabeth Bennet an offer of marriage under any circumstance.

I was absolutely taken aback. How did she find out? Or… rather, this was to make sure I did not do anything and not because she knew I had already done so. Still, it puzzled me that she knew something of my business and it annoyed me that she had an opinion on it.

Even though I was not ever going to listen to my aunt's insane demands, it irked me to have her make them in the first place. And annoyed me further to know I was the topic of gossip for her spies.

Could I not live my life as my own without interference from other people? Or was I going to be always at their beck and call because they believed to know better. Wanted what was best for me without ever asking me once what I wanted.

Then word reached my ear that she had called upon Miss Elizabeth Bennet.

I fumed at this. This was completely unacceptable! The meddling this woman was doing… how did she think it was going to end?!

Miss Elizabeth, by all accounts that I heard, had been headstrong and defiant.

My aunt had left not an hour later in a fit.

Lord, I wished I had been there to witness it.

But it did bring up a thought. Perhaps there was reason to still hope. If Miss Elizabeth had not bent to my aunt and promised to refuse any offer of marriage I could make… did that mean…? Could it be that she had changed her opinion of me?

Even while at Pemberly, when she had been more receptive to spending time in my presence, I had not dared to allow myself to hope for such a thing.

Now?

Yet, I did have a different matter to settle first. Before I could call upon Miss Elizabeth, I still needed to speak with Bingley.

*

Netherfield. Bingley had made a good choice in the property, I must admit. It was charming. Even more so when it was just us travelling to it and not with the sisters.

Bingley, ever the proper gentleman, made sure that we called upon the neighbours. That is, the Bennet family. We sat in their sitting room and suffered through one of the most excruciating teas in history.

Mrs Bennet hardly allowed anyone else to speak. Her distaste for me ever clearer with each sentence that came from her mouth. Snide comments, making clear she believed I did not act how a gentleman was supposed to act. That I should not have returned to the county was implied throughout.

Miss Elizabeth was a saving grace. My focus settled on her upon entering the room and I tried to look for any hint of encouragement. She smiled and acted… nervous.

She did try to engage Bingley in a conversation not dominated by her mother. But failed.

We left.

Bingley sighed when we had made it back to the road to Netherfield. "I can't believe I'd been in the same room as her again," he lamented.

Neither could I.

I cleared my throat. "Remember at Pemberly when I said I had a matter to discuss with you once everything was settled?"

He rocked in his saddle and looked at me funny. "Distinctly. I have been waiting on you to be in the right mood to bring it up. Is now the time?"

I nodded. "You can hate me for this, I will not blame you."

"What is it, man?!"

"I was wrong about Miss Jane Bennet. She does have a great amount of affection for you. What I perceived to be disinterest was her being shy. Not only that, I knew that she was in London and had called upon your sister, Miss Bingley. Yet I withheld that information from you. I am sorry." There. Truth exposed.

Bingley drew his horse to a sharp halt and gaped at me. "You knew she was in town?!"

"Yes."

"And that she had feelings for me?"

"On that, I learned only recently. But still, I interfered when I should not have."

"So that means..." he looked back the way we had come. "That means..."

I smiled, recognising this love-struck look. The beaming smile. The utter hope on his face. Eagerness to race back and to be in her presence once more. "Go."

He turned back to me. "And you approve?"

That shocked me. I expected him to yell and cast me out of his house or to at least give me a cold shoulder from now on. But no, he wanted my approval.

"Do you need it?" I asked.

He shook his head. "No. But I would like it, from my friend."

I reached across and slapped his shoulder. "You have it. Now go!"

No more hesitating, he spurred his horse into action and raced back to the Bennet house.

*

The next day, I joined Bingley as he called upon his fiancé. Luckily, a walk into Merriton was suggested and we all escaped the house.

Elizabeth walked by my side, slowing down ever so and creating a gap between us and the others ahead.

"Mr Darcy, I must be selfish and for the sake of my own feelings bring up this topic that will undoubtedly make you uncomfortable," she started. "I must thank you on behalf of my family for what you did for my poor sister, Lydia. Were it known to the rest of my family, they would be grateful and communicate that to you. Please do not be angry. And do not blame my aunt. It was Lydia who betrayed that you were concerned in the affair. My aunt only confirmed after I wrote to ask her about it," she cut a shy look at me sideways.

"I do not deserve the thanks," I was feeling all too self-conscious of it. She was not meant to know about my part in this.

"But you do!" she exclaimed. "You have been so kind to my family. We could never repay the debt. And… none of them know about your true involvement. So, I must be allowed to thank you on their behalf."

I hesitated. I did not want her family to be grateful to me… nor did I want her to feel indebted. "Do not thank me on their behalf. I did what was the right thing to do and expect nothing in return. Thank me for yourself if you must," I added as I noticed her starting to open her mouth to argue once more. "But know, I do not want you or your family to feel like you must pay me back a debt. Ever. You have no obligation to me at all."

She sighed. "I can assure you, I do not feel obligated to you."

Then what do you feel?

I swallowed and dredged up all my courage. "Miss Bennet… I…" I muttered a curse under my breath. "You are too generous, Miss Bennet, to trifle with me. Please, if your feelings are the same as they were last April, tell me so at once. Because my affections and wishes are… unchanged." I let out the words and hoped that this time, this would end different. "But," I reassured her. "One word from you will silence me on this subject forever."

"My feelings," she covered her mouth with her hand and looked everywhere but at me. "My feelings are…" Finally, she focussed on me, looked at me directly. "I am ashamed to remember what I had said then. But my feelings are very much different. In fact, they are the same as yours," a smile pulled at her lips and her eyes glimmered in the sunlight.

I mirrored her without realising. My mouth turning upward as I fully comprehended her words. She… she had feelings for me and was not rejecting.

I breathed out and searched for a topic that I could chat about with all these butterflies fighting in my chest to escape and fly out of my mouth.

"Lady Catherine visited you; I am told."

She laughed lightly.

"It gave me hope. That if you had absolutely decided against me you would have acknowledged it to her."

"Yes, you know enough of my frankness to know me to be very much capable of that," she laughed. "After abusing you to your face, surely I would have no issue with abusing you to all your relations."

"And what did you say to me?" I asked her. "Though formed on mistaken premises, it was nothing but the truth of the time. My behaviour had been unpardonable, I can hardly blame you for your response. 'Had you behaved in a more gentleman like manner'… you know not how those words have tortured me."

"I had no clue that they would have been taken in such a way," she admitted.

"I can understand. You thought me to be completely devoid of every proper feeling, I am sure you did. And then you told me that there was no way in which I could have addressed you that would have induced you accept my proposal."

"Do not repeat those words," she protested.

I grimaced as I mentioned the letter. "I knew that what I wrote to you in my letter would have caused you pain to read it, but I felt I needed to explain. Though," I swallowed hard. "I do hope it has been destroyed since."

"It will be," she promised immediately. "If that is what you wish, I will burn it as soon as I return home."

I chuckled at how serious she was. Touched by it. "Thank you."

"And please forget what mean words I spoke to you," she pleaded in return.

"But I needed to hear them. I needed to learn from them. I have always been a selfish being all my life. As a child I was taught what was right but not taught a good temper. Being the only son and an only child for so long meant my parents were very indulgent with me. And this taught me to be selfish and to care for only those within my immediate family circle. To think meanly of the rest of the world. Such I was from eight to twenty-eight. And such I might be had it not been for you. Without you, I would still be the same." I offered her my hand.

She slipped hers into mine and squeezed.

"Dearest Elizabeth. Please, may I be permitted to speak with your father and ask him to give his blessing for us to be wed?"

"Yes," she immediately said. "Yes, please hurry and do so."

*

Mr Bennet was surprised by my visit and even more so by my request for his daughter's hand in marriage.

"Lizzie? My Lizzie?"

I cleared my throat. "Yes, sir."

That startled him enough for him to remember his manners and clear his own throat. "Right. I guess my answer is yes, you have my blessing. But only after I speak with my daughter."

I could have sagged with relief! I nodded, knowing that Elizabeth wanted this too. That this being his only condition was more than reasonable. It was a lovely idea!

"Thank you, sir."

"Yes, well. I must confess that I am confused as to how this happened."

*

"How," Elizabeth demanded from me as we walked the garden of her home. "Did you come to love me? I could have sworn you did not have any feelings of affection for me."

"Is that why you acted surprised at Rosings?"

"Yes," she admitted with her usual frank honesty. "I never suspected."

"Good. I did not want you to."

"So how?" she pushed.

Sighing, I chose to tell her the truth. That it had been slow and grew with every interaction until I could not deny that I felt something for her. Also, that many of my close friends and family pointed out my own idiocy and encouraged me to act upon it, before it was too late. "And you?"

She smiled. "Pemberly."

"My house made you fall in love with me?"

She threw her head back and laughed. "It is a lovely house."

"I should have known," I played along. "You're only interested in my ten thousand a year."

She slapped my arm to chastise me. "Shh!"

We turned at the end and started the slow amble back towards the house.

"But really, it was at Pemberly when I realised that you were… not who I had thought you to be. Seeing your home, hearing how your staff were happy in their treatment from you and your family. Talking with you… Lord, I was so nervous then."

"So was I."

"The great Mr Darcy was nervous?! Never!"

I chuckled at that. "You'd be surprised, madam."

*

I took great pleasure in penning my aunt a response. This one was most certainly not an invitation for her attendance to my wedding. Nor was it an invite for her opinion. She was informed of my proposal to Miss Elizabeth Bennet and her acceptance of said offer.

When the Collins's arrived at Longbourne to give their congratulations, they mentioned Lady Catherine's displeasure in learning of our impending nuptials. It seemed they had to escape Rosings Park to be out of range of her anger.

*

We married alongside of Bingley and Jane. Family and friends filling the church at Longbourne.

I kissed my wife, leaning down while she reached up and tilted her chin to get closer. It was warm and felt… safe. My wife. The woman I would be taking to Pemberly to be mistress of my home. And to be the mother of my children.

Good heavens… children. We could very well have them by this time next year. Or rather one at least.

We bid our guests goodbye and climbed into our waiting carriage. Giddy to think of the future we were going to have together.

The next major milestone for each couple would be the wedding night. Bingley was taking Jane back to Netherfield, where they would live for the time being.

Elizabeth and I were travelling onwards to Pemberly. A long journey. But it would be well worth it to be home. And to have our complete privacy.

We talked on the ride… and shared heated kisses and touches the whole way. But we were careful. This was not an event to occur in a moving carriage.

*

I watched my wife closely as I closed the door to our bedchamber. Her eyes were darting around the room, never lingering long on any one thing. Completely avoiding the large bed. She fidgeted with her skirt.

"Elizabeth," I drew her attention. The use of her Christian name still felt intimate.

"Yes, Fitzwilliam?" she answered in turn. A flush of red staining her cheeks as she looked at me.

"We don't have to do anything you are not ready for," I reassured. Of course, this was going to be a challenge for me too, the first woman I would have taken to bed.

At this, she lost her innocent look and glared at me. "I want to be your wife!"

"You already are," I frowned. Did we not just get married in a church? In front of all our friends and family?

"In all…" she bit off, dropping her voice. "Sense of the meaning," she lowered her gaze to the floor.

Oh.

She wanted… I thought I was going to be dealing with a squeamish miss, not a woman who knew what she wanted.

She wanted to make love.

She wanted this.

She wanted me.

And in that moment, I cursed my pride from years before. I should have sought out a partner other than… well, other than the one other person I had loved and laid with. More experience on my part, especially with women, would mean I could give my wife an enjoyable wedding night.

For now, I was going to have to listen to her and do everything that pleased her.

"Fitzwilliam?"

Damn it, I had been standing there like a fool! "I am sorry," I said. "I was lost in my thoughts."

"Hopefully good thoughts?" she attempted to smile, but it was not as light hearted and carefree as she was trying for.

"I…" I stumbled over the words. Come on! She is your wife, be honest with her!

No. Not that honest. Nope. Honest with an erring side of prejudice. Yes.

"I do not want to disappoint you," I blurted out.

She sighed, her shoulders relaxing and a real smile curving her lips. "I do not want to disappoint you," she admitted.

I crossed the room and stood before her.

That night, we undressed each other. The sight of her feminine figure did not disappoint me. The sight of me did not send her fleeing the room.

We held each other. Kissed. Touched. When we made love, I shuddered and with hoarse whispers told her I loved her. She clung to me.

In the light of the morning, we snuggled. "Mrs Darcy, good morning."

"Hmmm, good morning, Mr Darcy…" she stretched lazily in my arms. "Fitzwilliam," she added on. "I like that better."

"You do?" I murmured into her temple and dropped several kisses there.

She nodded. "I have always called you Mr Darcy. But now I have the privilege of using your Christian name and knowing that only family get to use it."

I smiled at that. My fingers traced slow over her bare shoulder. "Lizzie," I tried out.

She flushed at that but kissed me anyway, so she must have liked it.

I was in heaven. This woman was now my wife. And it had been a love match. A woman who I could depend upon, who could depend upon me. "I am lucky to have you," I told her as I rolled and settled once more between her beautiful full thighs.

She gasped and squeezed them against my waist. "Prove it," she licked her lips. "Prove it to me now."

Rising to the challenge in more ways than one, I did just that. Gentle rocking, making sure to listen and watch for any sign of discomfort. Enjoying the way she gasped and hooked her leg over my hip and dug her heel into my lower back.

I worshiped her. Kissed the column of her throat, leaving bites when I discovered she would shudder and groan when doing so. Opened my mouth and enjoyed her tongue eagerly invading and seeking out mine.

Perfect bliss.

I wanted this to last forever, to keep her locked up in this room with me with no contact with the outside world ever again.

Who cared about that anymore when I skimmed my fingers over my wife's skin, then, at her guidance, went lower. The location of her bundle of nerves that brought her to completion and had her cling and claw my back as I rubbed on it over and over and over until she shuddered.

"Fitz… William," she gasped brokenly.

Hearing my name on her lips sent me over the edge and I spilled deep inside of her. Hips grinding to push it in as far as I could on instinct.

Then we were kissing soft and giggling at all this like the pair of love-sick fools we were.

Chapter Fifteen; Happily, Ever After

One year later…

Bingley purchased a property near Pemberly. Both Jane and Lizzie loved this. They were constantly in and out of each other's homes. And I liked having my friend close by to converse with. It was a good arrangement.

Bingley announced first. A month later, we were happy to announce too.

Babies. Our homes were going to be filled with children and they would be running from one home to another for forever. It would be lovely. I was so happy. So pleased.

Lizzie struggled to keep me sane and to stop me from talking to her belly as we laid in bed. Because, and I quote 'you talk to the baby more than you talk to me.' She had pouted. But with a soothing kiss and making sure she was very much aware of my love and affection for her, she relented. Reclined on the pillows and twirled her fingers through my hair as I marvelled at her growing belly.

At the end of the year, we welcomed our daughter into the world.

She was perfect. Tiny. I was afraid to hold her at first, afraid I would hurt this fragile being with my clumsy hands. But as soon as she nestled against my chest, right over my heart, that was it. They had a hard time getting me to release her to anyone.

"Lizzie," I cried to her. "Thank you."

She nodded and accepted that she was no longer the only woman I loved so whole heartedly in this world.

Everyone came for her Christening. Mr and Mrs Bennet, Kitty and Mary. Bingley and Jane and their tiny babe came to the church. Mr and Mrs Gardiner (to whom I am forever indebted because without them, Lizzie and I would never have married). Even my aunt, Lady Catherine, appeared.

Georgiana was happy to have a niece and cooed over her non-stop.

We were tempted to give her my mother's name, but chose not to. Enough members of my family shared names.

Instead, we gave her a name that was her own.

Simone Darcy.

Our party congregated back in our home so they could all have a turn meeting her. And congratulating Lizzie for bringing her into the world. Everything was perfect and as it should be.

And because my life is ridiculous and likes to make things hard for no reason, we had unexpected late comers to the house.

Mr and Mrs Wickham's arrival was a shock.

If I thought he looked terrible when last I saw him in London for his wedding… he was worse now. My stomach fell.

He stumbled into the sitting room we were all in and looked around, but his eyes never made contact. Lydia had her head held high and announced her presence loudly. Only her mother was eager to rush over and see her.

Lizzie shifted beside me, uncomfortable. I reached over and squeezed her hand reassuringly. Nothing would happen under our roof, I would make sure of that.

I looked over to Georgiana who was sat with Mrs Gardiner and my cousin. She pulled into herself, I watched as her shoulders rounded.

My cousin positioned himself in front of her so that she could not see George, and he shot me a concerned look.

Lord above.

I rose up and walked over to the Wickhams. Finally, George's eyes latched onto me and clung. "Darcy! Congratulations on the baby!" his voice was loud. He wobbled in place as if he were on a boat in rough seas.

Was he drunk?

I looked over my shoulder to the party that was watching us closely. Whatever I decided to do here would colour our relationship for the rest of our lives. If I welcomed them in, they would be welcomed by the rest of the family. But certain ones would want to know why I was doing so now. If I turned them away, most would agree with my decision.

But I was not ready to choose yet.

I needed to know why, after so long, George had decided to come. "Let's talk, in private." I allowed him no choice in the matter and placed a firm hand on his shoulder, shoving him back through the door.

He stumbled but moved without complaint.

Lydia tried to follow.

"Go to your sister, Lydia," I told her.

She frowned. "George?" she asked.

He waved over his shoulder at her. "Go have fun," he sang out.

I got us to the study and closed the door before even daring to take a full breath. When I turned, I found him at the side table pouring drinks. "Stop, George," I went over and took the glass from him before he could taste it.

He whined. "Just a little."

"You're acting like a drunk," I protested.

He snorted. "Acting? Ha! Give me the glass, Darcy."

"No," I downed it myself to get it away from him. Hissing at the sudden burn, I glared at him. "What are you doing here?"

"What do you mean? I am here to meet my new niece!"

"Don't give me that horse shit," I snapped at him. "I haven't seen you since your wedding day."

He flinched at that. "You made it clear then, Darcy, that you never wanted to see me again."

Damn it. "Since when have you ever listened to me?" I fired back, defiant.

He snorted at that. "I use to listen to you a lot," he dropped his voice and leaned in close. "Every sound you use to make for me."

Oh. A shiver ran through my body. This was bad. How did he manage to do that to me? I stepped away. "You're a drunk."

"Sure am." While I was distracted, he snatched the glass from my hand and poured himself another.

I shook my head. "Why?"

"Why what?" he asked as he gulped down his drink.

"Why are you doing this to yourself?" I waved my hand at him in general. The overall disarray of him was unmissable. "You look like shit."

"Thank you, Darcy. You are so sweet," he sarcastically shot back. "What else am I supposed to do?"

"What does that mean?"

He shrugged. "My life is a mess. My wife is so clingy it is suffocating. A little drink," he shook the glass to highlight it, amber liquid sloshing over the edge and ran over his fingers. "Helps me bear it." On that note, he tossed back the rest and sighed in relief.

"You're killing yourself like this," I said plainly.

"So?"

No.

I punched him.

He stumbled back, dropped his glass to the carpet, and yelled. "What the hell is wrong with you?"

"You are not going to die, you idiot!" I yelled back.

"What do you care?!"

"Stop saying I would not care! I care about you George! Always have! And I am not going to sit back and accept this! Get your shit together and live your damn life!"

"Why? What is so great in my life that I should even bother?!" he shook his head. "I'm not like you. I don't have a wife I can tolerate or a child I could give everything up to love. I'm not joking when I say my life is a mess."

"So change it!"

"What?!" he stared at me like I was the fool in this argument. Like I had lost all sense. "I can't very well get up and do that!"

"Then you're planning on drinking yourself to death, instead? That is not the George Wickham I know."

"The George Wickham you knew never existed! I've always been this way. You never wanted to see it."

Maybe he was right. But I wasn't going to stop. He was… he was my brother-in-law now. Family. I had to do something, it was expected and… Damnation! "I will pay for you to go and study if that is what you would like to do. I can give you land to work. I can…"

"Fitz," he stopped me. "I'm not your responsibility now."

"You always will be, George," I did not hesitate to say that. "Even if I want to give you a thrashing right now, you are my responsibility. You are my family."

"Darcy," he scoffed.

"My wife's brother-in-law," I clarified.

There. He clenched his jaw as if he was grinding his molars to crack. "Fuck off."

"Grow up," I snapped back. "I will always care for you and do what needs to be done to make sure you and your wife are provided for."

He rolled his eyes. "And how does your wife feel about such dedication to someone she doesn't even like? Hmm? Wouldn't she prefer you abandon your connection to me?"

"Lizzie trusts my judgment," thank goodness. But this would hurt her. And Georgiana. Why on Earth did he come back?!

He said nothing, stood there in the middle of the study, staring at the floor. The fight was leaving my body and I leaned against the edge of my desk.

Then he spoke and it was… painful, only because it was coming from him. "You love her," George's wounded look hurt me more than any blow could.

"Yes," I admitted.

It's the same. The same love I felt for George. Felt… Yes, past tense.

A humourless ha and George looked away. "I guess this really does make us brothers."

I hated that. It roiled in my stomach and made me ill to think that was all we would ever be. I stood up straight from the desk.

Not that I desperately wanted to claim George. No. I loved my wife. But… brothers should not love the way we had…

I took his wrist, drawing George's attention back to me.

"Fitz?"

No thoughts. No reasoning. I leant in, breath grazing over his lips, eyelids dropping to half-mast. So close. I was so close to kissing him once more.

"Fitzwilliam?" the door opened and Elizabeth froze.

I turned wide eyes to my wife.

What the devil…

Lizzie gaped at me.

George regained his senses first, amazing considering how pickled his brain must have been. Leapt back and yanked his wrist from me. "We were arguing," he cleared his throat. "That is all. Lydia and I will leave right now," he went to push past her through the doorway.

But she blocked him, stepped into the room and closed the door. This time, she locked it. "That was not arguing," she accused.

"I'm sorry. Lizzie," I started to beg. "I'm so sorry."

"For what?" she demanded.

George leapt in again. "For nothing. Nothing happened. He's in love with you! Nothing was happening."

She slapped him across the face and we all fell silent in the wake of it.

"I have eyes, George Wickham. And what I saw was not nothing," she turned to me. "I deserve an explanation."

George looked to me in panic. I could see now all those years of fear of being discovered and what it could mean and what it could result in for us. And the worst thing… I had so much more to lose than George did.

He hated his life. Was actively drinking his away.

But I had a wife. A child. I was happy.

Dear God… what had I done? Almost done? We didn't… I hadn't… Had I been going to…

"Fitzwilliam?" she brought me back to reality with her gentle hand on my cheek.

When had she crossed the room?

When had I started to cry?

I flinched and swiped at my tears in shame. "I'm sorry. I was being weak. We didn't do anything. We really were just arguing and then… we almost. But we didn't. I swear. I'm sorry."

She shushed me and drew me into a hug. "Talk to me, Fitzwilliam. What is going on here?"

I collapsed into her and held on tight. "You're going to hate me if I start talking."

Her arms tightened around me. "Let me decide that for myself."

"Fitz," George warned. "Don't."

She released me and glared at him. "Again, Wickham, I deserve an explanation."

"This isn't something that a wife needs to know. Or anyone else for that matter," he snapped back.

"Please, George," I begged him. "Let me fall on this sword myself."

He cursed and went back to the liquor. Now I wanted to join him in that.

She drew me to the lounge and held my hands. I tried to start, tried to find the words but failed. All the years I had wanted to tell another living person of this love affair so that it existed outside of us, and yet now my tongue failed.

Even if I followed George's lead and tried to hide it, this distance that had appeared between Lizzie and I would always be in our marriage.

I had lost George. And now I was losing Lizzie. When will my life not be about losing the people I love?

"Fitzwilliam, you're scaring me," she said.

"I love you but at the same time," oh Heavens… I still… Lord I am still an idiot! "I love George. I cannot explain it. Even after everything, I cannot stop feeling these feelings for him."

George slumped into a chair away from us and hid his eyes from me behind his hand. "Fuck Fitz."

"Everything I told you," I continued. "Was a half-truth. George and I did grow up together, but something changed and we fell in love. I have spent all my life loving him. When we were in university, George made a reputation to protect us. He became this rake who would flirt and seduce any and all women."

She looked at George in stunned silence.

He looked up and raised his glass to her in cheers. Then sank lower into the chair.

"He did try to elope with Georgiana," I admitted.

George shot up straight at that admission. "You told her about that?!"

I glared at him. "Of course, I did," I snapped. Then back to her I added, "But it wasn't for her dowry. He was trying to tie himself legally to my family so we would always be above suspicion. I could not hurt my sister nor could I share him with her. We parted ways after that and I never expected to see him again, least of all in Hertfordshire."

"Trust me, I felt the same," he added in his commentary.

"We never tried anything since. It was over between us," I told her. "When I went to London to discover him and Lydia, I went to make him marry her. And God, it hurt to be there for that." I swallowed. "I am not lying when I say I love you, Lizzie. And I cannot explain how it is that I can love two people like I do, it just is."

We lapsed into a silence once more.

"Lizzie?" I prompted her.

She squeezed my hands. "Let me think."

I nodded.

But George grumbled. "This is a mistake. You're a damned idiot, Darcy! Why did you have to spill all that?!"

"Because she's my wife," I snapped back.

"We're going to hang for this and you gave her all the evidence she needs to punish us."

"Hang?" she looked confused.

George glared at her. "Yes. What we did is punishable by death. What? Did you think we were hiding because we wanted to make it more exciting sneaking around? The worst-case scenario for us is death… best case is we run away to Europe." He looked to the heavens. "And honestly, that's sounding like a great plan right now."

"You still love him?" she asked George.

After a moment, he lowered his chin and looked me directly in the eye. "Never stopped."

Oh. My heart clenched at that. Even as my world was falling apart it felt good to know that he still loved me back.

Lizzie rose from her seat and withdrew her hands from mine. "I won't speak of this to anyone," she reassured us.

"You have my word. But I need time to think about all this."

"Lizzie," I did not know what to say.

"Mrs Darcy," he rose up. Addressing her so high-lighted an impossible truth that could not be denied; she was my wife. She was legally bound to my family. "If you can forget all this has happened, Lydia and I can leave right now and never return again. I swear. I will never come back to Pemberly."

She did not fidget. Did not hesitate. Like a true lady, she simply said, "Do not make any rash decisions. I need to think first. Then we can talk further." With that, she left the study.

George still looked ready to take his wife and run.

"It is better to do as she says," I told him. "Please don't leave Pemberly before she has time to think."

The muscles in his jaw tightened and then relaxed. "Fine. But this is a mistake."

George and Lydia stayed with us that night along with many other guests. My cousin tried to corner me to know why I was allowing them to stay. Funny, wasn't he the one telling me that it would not be unexpected for me to accept George back to Pemberly only a year ago?

Georgiana was uneasy around them. The Gardiners did not know what to make of it all. Bingley had offered to take them to his home, the good man he was.

I brushed them all off, too tired to deal with any of it, and unsure how I was supposed to respond.

Instead, I spent my time in the nursery with Simone. This might be the last chance I got to hold her, tell her I loved her, hear her cry. And I was not going to miss a moment of it. I would cherish this time.

The next morning, I looked about the same as George did. I did not sleep at all.

Lizzie called us to the study.

We marched in as if we were about to meet the executioner. She locked the door. At this point, I do not know if this was her subtle way of mocking us because we were caught because of an unlocked door. Or if she was remembering to do it so we had privacy.

George stood by my side.

"Don't look so worried," she said.

We both shared a confused glance before focussing on her again.

She sank to the chair and waved for us to take the lounge together. "I have spent the night thinking about this situation we're in and I have a solution that will be beneficial to all of us."

What on earth was she talking about?

"I understand that nothing that we discuss today can ever be shared with anyone outside of this room," she continued. "Very few would understand, and most would shame us for it."

"Lizzie," I tried to ask for her to clarify. But she held up her hand to halt my words.

She focused on George. "I will not be the one to send you to the gallows or force you to flee England and live in exile. I swear that."

"Then… what?" he shifted nervously. "What are we here to discuss?"

"I am making an offer to open our marriage," she looked to me and then back to him, "to be able to include you."

My heart stopped. I was dead. Must have been. Because the words coming from my wife's mouth hardly made any sense to me.

"Fitzwilliam loves us both. I want him to be happy and I am willing to share him with you, with conditions."

George fell back into the lounge and laughed in a light airy manner, like he was in the same disbelief I was in. "Are you… are you real? Are you not disgusted by us?"

She shook her head. "You're not the only ones to have loved someone you are not meant to." She allowed that one sentence to hang in the air for a moment before continuing.

That is when I realised that my wife and I shared something more in common. I wanted to ask her who she was referring to, but I also wanted to make sure this was real and that she was in truth giving me the ability to… to…

"I have conditions, George. And if at any time you fail to meet even one of them, I will close this marriage."

His spine shot up straight and he nodded at her. Suddenly full attention and focus. "Yes."

She smiled. "You must provide for Lydia."

His shoulders went up and I watched as his jaw clenched.

Lizzie shook her head. "You do not have to love her, but she needs a home and the protection of your name. You need to make sure she is taken care of… but you are not to share her bed anymore."

He nodded at this. "I can do that."

I blinked at him in shock. "Really?"

He glared at me. "I have not been in her bed in months. And might I remind you that I never enjoyed taking women to bed either. My preference has always been…" he trailed off and looked at Lizzie apologetically. "Pardon."

She laughed. "No, this is leading to my next condition. We have to talk. And make decisions together. No more making choices on your own, George. From the sounds of it, you did that a lot. It stops now and we must all agree. Together. Or not at all."

He swallowed hard. "I made those decisions for a reason."

"George," she warned him.

A battle of will between the two. But she won, once I reached over and touched his arm. He had relented and nodded in agreement. "Fine."

"And my final condition," she added. "You have to stop drinking, George. I do not think Fitzwilliam would survive losing you for good."

"I can do that," he promised.

She smiled at me. "Looks like you get to have both of us."

"Why are you doing this?" I asked of her.

She shook her head. "I cannot have Charlotte the way I want, in my life. So, let me give you this," she stood and came over and planted a kiss to my lips. "Let me share you with someone else."

I reached cupped her face and kissed her back. "Thank you," I whispered against her lips.

She smiled and nodded to George and left us alone.

George stared after her. "Did that really happen?"

I blinked back at him. "I dearly hope it did." And without restraint I crashed into him and kissed him for the first time in years.

But he pulled away. "Hold it, Fitz. We have to lock the door."

*

Publicly, we reconciled over our differences. George Wickham was forgiven for all that he had done. He was now welcomed at Pemberly.

Not everyone understood, but they learned to accept it. Though they treated George cordially, some relationships were strained. This we accepted. Georgiana got over her embarrassment and treated George like a brother once more. Colonel Fitzwilliam was more hesitant to accept. Lady Catherine was disappointed and demanded the man be cut off immediately. She was once again ignored.

George moved to one of the cottages on the grounds of Pemberly. For a time, he simply existed without expectations or profession. He left the military and lived off of an allowance that I gave him.

Lydia disliked this. She spent much of her time back at Longbourne with her mother or with her old friends she had made in the militia. Occasionally she would visit Jane or Lizzie.

I would spend many hours with George going about Pemberly and looking in on the tenants. And many hours in his cottage… where he chose to have only a housekeeper come in the morning to clean and cook for him. The rest of the time, it was a private sanctuary for us.

Lizzie and I had more children.

Our daughters came to rival the number of Lizzie's sisters. So much so, she tried to banish me from our marital bed. That did not last long, though we did take precautions to prevent any more pregnancies.

I had Lizzie and I had George.

I was happy.

Hello

Thank you for reading Fitz.
I hope you have enjoyed it!
Please leave an honest review wherever you like to do
that, share with a friend, and go drink some water!!!
Thank you,
April

Independently published author. Artist. BL and fanfic whore. April Klasen lives in regional Australia. Find her @defiantdame on most social media sites or sign up for the book newsletter to stay up to date with new stories.

Book Newsletter

Also by April Klasen

Blair: Salem's Daughter
Blair: The Sleeping Daughter
Blair: The Same Daughter
The Annual
Beta
Pure PopAsia
I Heart PopAsia
Summertime Madness
Hook-up or Date